C-NOTE

A DIFFERENT KIND OF LOVE

C-NOTE

A DIFFERENT KIND OF LOVE

The Unauthorized Biography

Elina Furman

BERKLEY BOULEVARD BOOKS, NEW YORK

C-NOTE: A DIFFERENT KIND OF LOVE

A Berkley Boulevard Book / published by arrangement with the author

PRINTING HISTORY
Berkley Boulevard edition / February 2000

All rights reserved.
Copyright © 2000 by Penguin Putnam Inc.
Book design by Carolyn Leder.
Cover photo by John Spellman/Retna Limited, U.S.A.
This book may not be reproduced in whole or in part,
by mimeograph or any other means, without permission.
For information address: The Berkley Publishing Group,
a division of Penguin Putnam Inc.,
375 Hudson Street, New York, New York 10014.

The Penguin Putnam Inc. World Wide Web site address is
http://www.penguinputnam.com

ISBN: 0-425-17336-4

BERKLEY BOULEVARD
Berkley Boulevard Books are published by The Berkley Publishing Group,
a division of Penguin Putnam Inc.,
375 Hudson Street, New York, New York 10014.
BERKLEY BOULEVARD and its logo
are trademarks belonging to Penguin Putnam Inc.

PRINTED IN THE UNITED STATES OF AMERICA

10 9 8 7 6 5 4 3 2 1

For all the C-Note fans

Contents

Acknowledgments		ix
Introduction	*C-Note: Looking Like a Million!*	xi
Chapter 1	Welcome to Orlando!	1
Chapter 2	Great Expectations	13
Chapter 3	Building a Pop Empire	23
Chapter 4	Basic Training	37
Chapter 5	Just Rewards	50
Chapter 6	David	67
Chapter 7	Dru	73
Chapter 8	Raul	79
Chapter 9	Brody	84
Chapter 10	Breaking Out	90
Chapter 11	The Star Connection	106
Chapter 12	Test Your C-Note IQ	114
Chapter 13	Cyber C-Note	119

Acknowledgments

I'd like to thank everyone who has helped me put this book together, including my editor, Tom Colgan, and Samantha Mandor for all their effort and dedication, and the greatest agent in the world, Giles Anderson. As always, my mother, Mira, for her support and encouragement. And none of this could have been possible without my sister Leah's assistance and meticulous attention to detail. Finally, I would like to thank John Nikkah for his invaluable assistance in the research department.

Introduction

C-Note: Looking Like a Million!

They came from a place called Orlando, Florida. A band of well-toned, sharply dressed guys packing voices powerful enough to start girls swooning with just one note. Some call them a band of musical outlaws, others just stare in amazement as they pass on by, wondering where they came from and how long they plan to stay. Those of you who are up on the late-breaking news know them as C-Note, and, if you've been following their invasion of the United States closely, you also know that they're here to stay.

With their first single, "Wait Till I Get Home," and their debut album, *A Different Kind of Love*, making mad waves all around the country, C-Note has shown the world that there's more to them than just good looks, dazzling smiles, and heart-stopping sex appeal. A sizzling new quartet who combines a full repertoire of fiery vocals with an enviable display of dance skills, C-Note moves effortlessly from smooth a cappella harmonies to deep R&B sounds, while incorporating a wealth of Latin-influenced rhythms.

While gearing up to make a lasting musical impact, the group underwent extensive training at the Trans Continental Records facility, the birthplace of both the Backstreet Boys and 'N Sync. From media and vocal training to dance rehearsals and image planning, the members of the group have been taking a crash course in pop stardom. Comprised of four young men—José "Brody" Martinez, Raul Molina, Andrew Rogers, and David Perez—C-Note has proven its musical mettle by selling out summer tours all over the country. After only a small sampling of this group's musical skills, fans were already anxiously awaiting the debut album and lining up to see them in person.

Boasting a unique combination of all-American good looks and Latino heritage, the foursome is glad to be embraced by teenagers from all backgrounds. With magazine covers, national talk shows, and huge summer concert tours with Brandy, Britney Spears, and Cher already under their belt, there's no doubt that C-Note will be making the country take note well into the new millennium.

C-NOTE

A DIFFERENT KIND OF LOVE

1

Welcome to Orlando!

When C-Note first appeared on the pop music scene, the fans couldn't make heads or tails of their mysterious emergence. While some people thought that the group had simply materialized out of thin air, others believed that C-Note was just hatched in the Trans Con incubator. From Orlando to Dubuque to Seattle, the question on everybody's lips was, "Where did C-Note come from?"

Like most success stories, the saga of C-Note has a beginning, a middle, and an end. After all, C-Note's vocal harmony, perfectly choreographed moves, and airtight stage shows could not have been built in one day. It would take many years of struggle and frustration for Dru, Brody, David, and Raul to come together as a group. And it would take even longer for them to find their way into the pantheon of pop stardom.

Through it all—the trials and tribulations, the struggles and defeats—the guys of C-Note never wavered in their goal of one day becoming the hottest singing group in the country. Their rise to stardom is a lesson in courage for everyone who has ever had the desire to pursue their wildest dreams until they turn into a reality.

CONNECT THE DOTS

While members of some singing groups meet at an audition, and are selected by judges to join the party, this was not the case with the guys of C-Note. Back when C-Note was just another name for a hundred-dollar bill, Dru, David, Brody, and Raul were already on a first-name basis. Of course, at the time, they were just beginning to make their way in the world. Many years would have to pass before the foursome finally came together as an official musical group.

If you happen to meet one of the guys and ask them how the group came to be, prepare yourself for a long and convoluted account. The truth is that making sense out of C-Note's history is like playing a game of connect the dots—you have to follow along very carefully if you want to get a clear image of what actually happened.

In one way or another, all of the guys knew each other before making their way to sunny Orlando, Florida. The first guys to meet were Raul and David. They were attending the same high school. But instead of trying out for the glee club, these guys were knee-deep into the game of basketball.

Raul and David were extremely close in those days, and even played on the same basketball team. The guys were two of the most talented players on the team. Little did anyone know, however, where their true talents would one day lie. As the star players of the basketball team, David and Raul hung out after school, double-dated, and perfected their slam dunks on the local courts. They were two of the most popular guys in their class, and stayed close friends throughout high school. But when the time came to graduate, the star athletes lost touch.

David was spotted by a scout during one game, and was offered a full academic scholarship. Unwilling to turn that down, he decided to devote the rest of his life to perfecting his game. Raul, however, was always torn between the worlds of music and sports. Basketball had meant a lot to him, but it would never replace the all-important role that singing played in his life. So when Raul was offered a music scholarship, he wasted no time in deciding to pursue a career as a singer.

Although the two amigos missed each other from time to time, their career choices couldn't have been more different. While David was off making baskets and running the court, Raul was busy tuning his vocal instrument. "David and I went to high school together—we actually didn't sing together, we played basketball together, stuff like that," Raul told *Soul Train* magazine. "When we graduated high school we went our separate ways—David in pursuit of basketball and I went into music."

With the common link of sports now broken, the guys thought that they had outgrown their friendship and that they'd never be able to connect like they had in the past. Boy, were they ever wrong.

THE DARING DUO

It was only a matter of time until two more C-Note members would come face-to-face with one another. Like Raul, Brody had been planning a career in music since he was just a toddler. Unlike Raul, however, Brody didn't stray from his course in high school by playing sports. By steadfastly working toward his ultimate dream, Brody won a music scholarship to a Florida college.

Soon after he arrived, destiny struck.

Brody met Raul in college and the two clicked instantly. Raul needed a new friend with the same common interests, and Brody seemed like the perfect choice. Both guys were of Latino descent and loved nothing more than singing in front of a crowd.

When they realized just how much they had in common, they were soon spending all their time together.

From their classes to their dorms, the two guys became virtually inseparable. And although they were involved in campus activities and the music department, Raul and Brody never lost sight of their life's ambition—to become famous singers. "Brody and I used to sit around and he would spend the night at my house," Raul recalled during an interview. "At three A.M., we would be listening to music and be like, 'We have to fly out tomorrow to meet Brian [McKnight] because we're going to do a song together. Diane [Warren] is writing a song for us and Janet [Jackson] wants me to do a song for her.' We could go on for hours and hours, acting like we were serious."

Dreaming about the future was one thing, but Brody and Raul had had enough of fantasy and wanted to experience the real thing. They were sure that if they could just find the right group of singers, they would be able to rise to the top. But confidence would only get them so far. Before they could hobnob with music industry veterans, they would have to put together a group and hone their skills.

To achieve that end, Brody and Raul set out on a marathon search for the perfect singing group. They auditioned students from their college and even put out ads in newspapers. Finding the right people turned out to be the easy part.

Keeping a group together would prove far more difficult.

Few singers had the dedication to stick it out during the lean years. As students, Brody and Raul had to study during the day and then devote their evenings to rehearsal. Sticking to the grueling schedule drained them of their energy, but somehow the guys managed. Sadly, the other members didn't fare as well and left the group when success failed to materialize.

STILL GOING STRONG

After forming one group after another, Brody was becoming more and more frustrated. Disillusioned by the music industry and fearing that he was wasting his time on the group when he should have been concentrating on his classes, Brody was at his wits' end. As difficult as it was to break the news to Raul, Brody knew that he would have to do it. Risking the friendship, Brody announced that he would be leaving the group in order to improve his grades.

Raul was very upset by Brody's departure. He had grown to rely on him for support, especially when everyone else seemed to consider his goals nothing more than foolish pipe dreams. But he understood that Brody was being pressured to improve his grades, and the two remained good friends despite the fact that they ended their professional relationship.

Even though Brody found it difficult to balance schoolwork with the responsibilities of launching a singing group, Raul was determined to make it work. Intent on becoming a success, he vowed not to let anything interfere with his goal. Of course, that didn't mean that he stopped trying to get good grades and keeping up with his schoolwork. On the contrary, he devoted as much time to his academics as he did to his singing group.

Now that he was on his own, Raul needed to find a new group to sing with. He auditioned for several, but had a hard time choosing the right group. Then he met Andrew "Dru" Rogers, who was destined to become the next member of C-Note, as well as a close personal friend.

Dru and Raul hit it off from the get-go. They had an instant rapport and found that the timbre of their voices gelled into a perfect harmony. When Dru's group asked Raul to join up, he was glad to accept the invite. "I got asked to audition for another group and it turned out to

be what Dru was in," Raul explained to *Soul Train* magazine. "So I met Dru and me and him sang together for
about six or seven months, almost eight months."

The time Raul spent in Dru's singing group was one
of the best of his life. He was glad to be in a group that
was just as committed to making great music as he was.
The guys worked very hard to gain recognition. But no
one worked harder than Dru and Raul. They went out
of their way to build a reputation around town, and even
tried to do charitable acts by singing at Catholic schools
and after-school programs for young kids.

Alas, that singing group was also doomed to fail. After the group broke up, Dru decided to move to Boston
to sing in yet another group with his brother. Raul would
not hear from him for another year.

All was not lost, however, because another twist of
fate would come along to bring the boys of C-Note
closer together. Brody had sworn that he had given up
singing in groups for good, but he couldn't resist the
lure of the spotlight. While Raul was off singing with
Dru, Brody had decided to make a comeback. Eventually, Brody called the one friend he could trust to support him.

Luckily, his call came just as Raul was in between
groups. Excited to reunite with his old pal, Raul welcomed Brody back like a prodigal son. The only problem was that two guys do not a group make. Raul and
Brody would have to start from scratch again. They went
back to the drawing board and worked hard to put together a new group, one that would stand the test of
time. "Brody called back and was like 'Hey I want to
start back into it,' " said Raul. "So then Brody and I
started putting another group together."

By this time, the guys had had just about enough of
the auditioning process, having been through it one too
many times. They had seen their share of performers
come and go, and tried to avoid the mistakes of their
past. Finally, when they believed they had found the

perfect group of singers, they synchronized their moves, harmonized their voices, and worked out their repertoire.

They were now ready to go public.

Although they had all the makings of a pop sensation, booking gigs was no easy task. Brody and Raul took it upon themselves to manage the group. What they didn't realize was just how tough finding work could be. For a vocal group, paying gigs were few and far between. Brody and Raul had to work overtime to audition for club owners and producers. But no matter how hard they worked, it seemed that the only jobs they could get were weddings and birthday parties.

THE MISSING PIECE OF THE PUZZLE

While playing at private parties seemed like a long way off from the MTV Music Awards, this type of job was actually more rewarding than Brody and Raul could ever have imagined. Not because they were being paid a ton of money—they weren't—but because they would finally hook up with one of the most pivotal parts of the C-Note puzzle.

What seemed like another routine birthday bash turned out to be one of the most important events in C-Note's history. Once Brody, Raul, and the rest of their gang showed up to sing at the soiree, they were pleased to discover that the party was being held for David's little sister—the same David that Raul had played basketball with in high school. The two friends couldn't have been happier to see each other. They'd missed each other more than either had realized, and seeing one another reminded them of all the good times they'd shared during their glory days in high school.

After catching up with his long-lost friend, Raul and the rest of the group proceeded to entertain the crowd. But no matter how hard they tried to get noticed, competing with David's smooth and sexy moves on the dance floor proved impossible. Watching David dance, they realized he had a natural gift for entertaining crowds. Everyone at the party had stopped to watch David groove on the dance floor. That's when Raul, Brody, and their group decided that if you can't beat 'em, join 'em—or recruit 'em, as the case may be.

They were so impressed with his showmanship, style, and look that they decided to ask him to audition for the group the next day. "I hadn't seen him since we graduated—and so we started talking and stuff," Raul told *Soul Train* magazine. "By the end of the night, me and him [Brody] always thinking about the group were like, 'you know what, we should ask him,' because he's got a deep bass voice we were looking for, and he was dancing and stuff, and he had the personality, so we were like let's ask him to join."

Although David had always loved dancing, he had never thought about singing for a living. But he couldn't resist the guys' entreaties. After all, what did he stand to lose? If the group liked him, he would join. If not, he would continue playing basketball. After being begged to audition for nearly an hour, David caved in and agreed to show up for the informal tryout. "I didn't take singing seriously until I met Raul at my sister's birthday party," explained David. "He asked me to audition for this previous group, I was like, 'Okay, I'll try out.' "

ON THE BRINK OF DISASTER

When David showed up for rehearsal the next day, he sang one song and showed off some of his latest dance steps. Right off the bat, Brody and Raul understood that David had exactly what the group needed—a funkier and more streetwise edge. David had an urban look that was all the rage, and even though he had never sung professionally, his voice had the deep bass they needed to round out the harmonies.

After talking it over for a couple of minutes, the group

came back with their verdict. David had been officially voted into the group. With the ball in his court, David had a decision to make. Could he dedicate himself to the group, or would he rather restrict his talents to dance floors and showers? Because his old friend, Raul, was so encouraging, David couldn't resist coming along for the ride. Maybe he did have what it took to become a widely known musical superstar. Once the idea of fame, wealth, and power embedded itself into his head, he was hooked, line and sinker.

But joining at the spur of the moment required that David accelerate the learning process. Raul, Brody, and the rest of the group had been singing and performing together for several months. They knew all the moves and had all the lyrics down pat. As the rookie of the bunch, David had to work full-time just to catch up with his new comrades. He worked so hard to perfect his voice and movements that in a couple of weeks a passing onlooker would never dream that he was new to the business.

With David on board, the group received a new surge of energy and creativity. Suddenly, they felt as if there was nothing they couldn't do if they put their minds to it. All this optimism made them work even harder to secure new jobs and find a manager. David was instrumental in helping the group spread the good word. He tacked up posters, cold called clubs, and went out of his way to attract attention.

Once several months had passed with nary a sign of progress, the group began to lose some of its motivation. They couldn't understand why they still had not received their big break. After all, they had the look and the sound. No matter how much they racked their brains, the guys could not come up with the solution to their woes.

Eventually, the lack of jobs and the long rehearsals took its toll on the group's morale. Although Brody, David, and Raul were just as committed to making it work, the other group members were already thinking about branching out on their own. Dissent and arguments among the singers were not uncommon, and Raul, Brody, and David decided to cut their losses. "That group broke up," said Raul, "but us three wanted to stay together and we were just thinking about what we were going to do."

DRU TO THE RESCUE

The last thing the three amigos wanted to do was to break in another rookie performer. The three of them had become so close that allowing a stranger into the fold seemed like a tremendous compromise. But no matter how hard they tried to put off the inevitable, there was no denying that a fourth voice was needed to complete the sound.

Brody, Raul, and David vowed that this would be their last audition. They would not let anyone in the group who couldn't be trusted. So instead of staging open calls for a new member, they decided to find someone through their network of friends. After calling distant relatives and acquaintances from the past, they still couldn't find the right person. That's where Dru came in.

Just as the guys were plumbing the depths of their pool of acquaintances, Dru had decided to move back to Orlando from Boston. He and his brother had been singing there for about a year, but when the group disbanded, Dru headed back to the sunny shores of Florida.

As the new kid in town, Dru was eager to touch base with some of his old friends. One of the pals on his list just happened to be Raul. Dru recalled the friendship with fondness, and couldn't wait for what promised to be a happy reunion. But when he finally caught up with Raul, Dru realized that his friend had been going through something of a rough patch.

When Dru came by to visit Raul, he met Brody and

David, who were just getting ready to begin rehearsal. "Dru had come by to say 'Hi' because he had come back into town from Boston," Raul informed a reporter. "And we used to work together, so he came back in to talk to everybody and say what's up and see what was going on. And they [Brody and David] still think that I set the whole thing up, but I didn't. It happened, it was real."

Judging by the dour looks on their faces, Dru could tell that trouble was afoot. When Raul, Brody, and David told him that they were struggling to find a new member, they never thought that Dru would want to join their group. To Raul, it seemed that Dru always had something going on. Even though he would have loved to invite Dru to join, Raul didn't want to pressure him into anything.

The trio had also been billing itself as a strictly Latin act, singing only in Spanish. The fact that Dru was not of Latino descent didn't mesh with their image. The idea that they could combine English and Spanish had just never occurred to them. Luckily, Dru saw the potential. "So then we all hit it off, we talked," recalled Raul, "and when he left the last thing he said was 'if you guys need anybody, if you need anyone to sing with—just call a brotha.' "

To their utter amazement, it was Dru who finally broached the issue of singing together. Because he didn't have his own group, Dru was only too happy to help out in any way he could. The offer was just too good to refuse. The three friends asked Dru to audition the next day. "Dru had just moved down from Boston," Raul told America Online. "Dru and I were in a group before that other one. And Dru had gone up to Boston to follow some other music stuff. And we all met and we all just kind of hit it off and asked Dru if he wanted to join the group and that was it."

Having sung alongside Dru for close to a year, Raul knew that he could hold his own vocally. The audition, therefore, was not set up to test Dru's singing ability, so much as to see whether his voice harmonized with their own. Choosing a song that they all knew, the four guys proceeded to belt out an a cappella number that knocked their socks off.

The year was 1995, and it marked the beginning of everything else. As Dru told the newspaper *Knight Ridder*, "The minute we sang together, we knew, 'This is it.' "

2

Great Expectations

C-Note had at last become an official group. Brody, Dru, David, and Raul knew that this time they were embarking upon a great adventure. They could feel it in their bones. Sure, each had been confident in his talents all along, but now that they were a team, there was simply no stopping them. "Not making it was never an option," Raul told *Latin Girl* magazine. "If you consider failure a possibility you are giving yourself an out. We never did that."

As soon as they joined forces, it seemed as if they had been destined to sing together. All four were gifted dancers, great lookers, and wonderful singers. They had the perfect combination of sex appeal, street savvy, and charisma. With Dru on board, the group could even boast a more mainstream image. But Brody, Raul, and David's Latino heritage would not take a backseat to Dru's all-American look.

Because the group wanted to reach as wide an audience as humanly possible, and satisfy the diverse tastes of each member, they made a collective decision to sing in both English and Spanish. One of the few groups ever to accomplish this feat, the guys of C-Note believed that this strategy would set them apart from the competition.

GETTING BY

With their bilingual image all carved out, the foursome's next step was to work out the kinks in their repertoire. That translated into work and more work. Since their singing careers weren't paying the bills, Brody, Raul, David, and Dru had to hold down part-time jobs while they waited for their big break. All told, the guys worked at countless odd jobs, such as hotel manager, girls' basketball coach, waiter, and even bus driver. Working nine to five sat none too well with the singers, who wanted nothing so much as to perform in front of an audience.

The guys devoted the little free time they did have to their music. As soon as the five o'clock whistle blew, they would gather to rehearse way into the wee hours. Of course, such a backbreaking regimen didn't leave much time for sleep. During their early years, in 1995 and 1996, C-Note was one of the most sleep-deprived groups in the entire country. David complained of their hardships to *Entertainment Weekly*: "For years, we would go to work, go to school, rehearse till three in the morning, then have to wake up three hours later for work again."

As tired and poor as they were, Brody, Dru, Raul, and David had never been happier and more determined to make it. As opposed to the group's former incarnations, when every setback caused a rift and every rift resulted in a breakup, the difficulties that this quartet encountered only served to bring them closer together. Raul spoke for the whole group when he said, "It's hard work and people tell you that you have to prepare for failure. In my head, I never thought about it. It was not an option to me and if it happened, then it happened. That was it— I tried. I was never like, 'Just in case I fail . . .' or, 'Just in case I can't do it . . .' There was never an idea in my head to fail. When it was going to happen and where it was going to happen were my only questions."

With that kind of attitude, it's no wonder C-Note eventually broke the success barrier. To contend with the hard labor and low pay that lined their road to fame, the guys of C-Note needed all the positive thinking they could get.

FRIENDS FOR LIFE

Part of why C-Note never lost steam during those lean years was because they had each other for support and motivation. Raul, Brody, David, and Dru had become a family, and knowing that they were a team gave them the courage to persevere. This was the first time that they had ever experienced such a great sense of camaraderie. The four musketeers' "all for one, and one for all" attitude helped forge a solid bond that still exists to this very day. "When you're friends first, you have that click," David told *Teen* magazine. "You know how when you get around certain people and you tell a joke and everyone gets it? Because of that, we have a lot of fun doing what we do."

Whenever one of the guys would become discouraged, the others would take it upon themselves to breathe new life into the enterprise, whether it was trying out for a new talent show or networking with a new producer or manager. Raul, Brody, David, and Dru felt that being in C-Note was their best chance for success, and they weren't about to take their careers or each other for granted.

The fact that they shared everything from their clothes to their hairstyling secrets to their rehearsal space wasn't the only basis for their friendship. All work and no play would make C-Note a dull group. They may have been burning the midnight oil by rehearsing their act and working during the day, but the group still found time to let loose and paint the town.

Whenever the guys would step out for a night on the town, they would get plenty of attention from everyone they passed. Who could resist staring at this well-dressed and diverse group of guys? Raul, David, Brody, and Dru never missed an opportunity to dress up and go dancing. And you can bet that wherever C-Note went, a crowd was sure to follow. "Not to be cocky," Brody revealed to *Teen* magazine, "but before we were signed or had a manager, any time we were together, heads turned."

Be they ever so humble, the guys of C-Note were irresistible to girls—even before they so much as sang one note. Working to get their careers off the ground may have been their top priority, but as red-blooded males, Raul, Brody, Dru, and David always made time for love and dating. Unfortunately, none of the guys had time to pursue a steady relationship. Save for a few month-long relationships here and there, the guys of C-Note could not find room in their schedules to experience what true love had to offer.

Of course, that didn't stop them from trying to do everything in their powers to impress the opposite sex. The guys always had tons of girls flocking to their corner, whether they were playing basketball, eating in a restaurant, or just heading out to the movies together. No doubt about it, this quartet was used to getting a lot of attention. But when the guys had set their sights on a special someone, they had no problem busting out the fancy footwork. Their standard operating procedure was to turn up the charm to full volume by serenading the objects of their affections. "We used to go to restaurants and eat, and if we spotted a good-looking girl or something, we would just walk over there and sneak up and ask if we could sing for them," Raul admitted to *Soul Train* magazine. "Like one of us and all the rest of us would join in, 'what's your name, what's your number?' hook it up."

THE BIG BREAK

As so many aspiring young singers and dancers already know, lightning can strike at any time in Orlando. The city was always bustling with energy, and local talent scouts have long been on the prowl for new groups. But the only way to get discovered was to showcase your skills at a talent agency, theme park, or to audition for a local show. So that's exactly what the boys of C-Note set out to do in the spring of 1997.

Checking the city magazines and newspapers for updates of musical events, talent shows, and festivals, Raul, Brody, David, and Dru kept up with all the latest developments on the Orlando music scene. They knew who was playing where and when, as well as which record execs were in town looking for new acts.

During one such routine perusal of their local paper, the boys discovered an ad for a local talent show. They were determined to win. Since they had improved their act considerably, C-Note's potential was unlimited. The years they'd spent together had seen them go from amateur night wannabes to one of the most polished and professional groups in Orlando. Now all Raul, David, Dru, and Brody had to do was win first place.

Although a nominal monetary reward would go to the winners, C-Note wasn't at all concerned with the small payment. They aimed to be discovered by a talent agent or a manager. Their victory would not be complete until they got their name in the paper and received the kind of recognition that would eventually earn them the ultimate goal—a recording contract.

For some curious reason, the boys had extremely high hopes going into the competition. While they had often performed at talent shows, even managing to place occasionally, this particular battle of the balladeers had them more excited than ever. Something told them that this time would be different, that this show would mean the beginning of a whole new chapter in their lives. "Something's going to happen," Dru conveyed to *Entertainment Weekly*. "Whether it's good or bad, we're gonna pull through it."

When the boys took to the stage, they could almost feel the adrenaline coursing through their veins. As they went through the motions of the all-too-familiar routine, the guys were on fire and the audience knew it.

Something in the way they sang, moved, and gestured to the crowd revealed that they were ready for bigger things. Those who watched the guys of C-Note on that fateful day will tell you about the magic that they created on stage. Their performance was nothing short of inspirational.

During their song, the crowd was amazed by the talented foursome. Of the hundreds of girls who'd come out for the event, many were crying and rushing up to the stage. Countless others were screaming and begging for an encore. The presiding judges had never imagined that a local singing group, with no reputation to speak of, could have such a profound effect on the audience.

After all of the other acts had had their chance to shine, it was time to announce the winners. The judges began by giving out the prizes for third and second place. Neither of those winners were C-Note. Raul, Brody, David, and Dru's anxiety was mounting by the second. Were they out of the running, or could it be that they were actually going to take first place for the first time in their lives? By the time the judges were ready to announce the winner of the talent show, the guys of C-Note were so nervous they could barely stand the suspense. But when they heard their names and the words "first place" spoken in one sentence, they jumped for joy, giving each other high fives. All the breathless anticipation had been worth it.

They had won the biggest talent show in the city of Orlando.

Raul, David, Brody, and Dru couldn't believe what

had just happened. As they posed for their pictures and raised their trophy in celebration, they felt as if all of their hard work had finally paid off. But before they could even begin thinking about the implications of their monumental victory, they were approached by a representative from Trans Continental Records.

The company that had brought us such multiplatinum artists as the Backstreet Boys and 'N Sync wasn't very well-known at the time, except to music industry insiders. When Trans Con came to woo C-Note, the Backstreet Boys and 'N Sync hadn't even broken in the United States. But the guys of C-Note knew all about the company and its renowned owner Louis Pearlman. "Trans Con actually came to us," Raul informed *Billboard* magazine. "Backstreet Boys hadn't happened here yet, and 'N Sync was just breaking in Germany."

They had heard about the international success of the Backstreet Boys and 'N Sync from some of their friends, and often wished that they, too, could hook up with someone like Pearlman.

So when the rep from Trans Con came by to congratulate the boys, the boys understood the magnitude of the impact that this meeting could have on their lives. The talent scout was extremely impressed with the group. He had gauged the full reaction of the audience, and was impressed with how professionally the members of C-Note handled themselves onstage.

He was also impressed with the Latin influences of the music. At the time, none of Trans Con's groups had ever tried to cross over into the Latin quarter of the music business. Sensing that this market was potentially very lucrative, the rep decided that bringing the boys aboard was in the company's best interest.

At first, the rep could barely get a word in edgewise. Raul, David, Dru, and Brody were just too excited. All four were practically falling over themselves to ingratiate the group into Trans Con's good graces. Little did they know that the battle had already been won.

Once the scout unveiled his thoughts on the future of the group's career, the guys couldn't believe what they were hearing. They had waited so long for this moment, and suddenly all their fantasies of finding a powerful manager were coming true. Was it real, or was this oasis of opportunity just another mirage?

After the agent handed them a card and asked them to come back for another meeting at the Trans Con headquarters, the guys could finally breathe a long sigh of relief. Their triumph was that much sweeter because they had gone through so many trials and endured so many struggles.

Looking at each other, the guys could only think of one thing to do and that was to celebrate. After yelling and jumping up and down for what seemed to be the hundredth time that day, the guys left the concert hall. But before they could really start the party, Raul, David, Brody, and Dru wanted to share the good news with their family and friends. Every time they shared the story with someone new, it became that much more concrete. They had to tell everyone.

After what seemed like many hours and dozens of calls, the guys regrouped to celebrate this life-altering event. They decided to spare no expense, and treated themselves to a great dinner at a fancy restaurant. Then, it was off to the clubs. No matter where they went or whom they told about the big news, the guys of C-Note had a permanent smile fixed upon their faces. They were just too happy for words, and the natural high lasted way past the morning hours.

SEALING THE DEAL

Once the morning came and the guys had a chance to look upon their situation with fresh eyes, they realized that their elation had yet to subside. But as with any great victory, the guys wanted to solidify the event, to put something in writing so they could finally rest easy.

Male versions of Cinderella, they worried that their carriage would turn into a pumpkin and their Prince Charming—in this case Louis Pearlman—would vanish into thin air.

To put their minds at rest, the guys quickly called up their contact at Trans Con and arranged to meet with the entire team. When the big day finally arrived, the boys made their way into the sprawling Trans Con facility. As they walked into the building, they felt as if they were about to make music history.

But first they would have to impress Louis Pearlman.

When the forty-something man walked into the room, the guys were awed by his formidable presence. That reaction, however, didn't stop the group from pulling themselves together and delivering a heart-stopping performance right then and there. After just one meeting, Louis Pearlman decided that he liked what he saw.

Once they concluded their short performance, the guys were led into Pearlman's commodious office. In the ensuing meeting, Pearlman explained the workings of the Trans Con family and what he and his team could do for C-Note's career. Whether the pop giant knew it or not, the guys had been sold on his company long before they had ever set foot on its premises. With every word that came out of Pearlman's mouth, Raul, David, Brody, and Dru became more and more excited. They could now quit their jobs and concentrate on their music full-time. "We were paying for our own vocal coaches and choreographers," Dru explained to the *Knight Ridder* newspaper, "They estimated all that and hooked us up with their own people. They gave us the means to better ourselves in music. We didn't have to work three or four jobs anymore."

They couldn't believe that everything would be paid for, from their choreographers to their vocal coaches to their clothes. And the idea of traveling the world to sing in foreign countries was even more thrilling. Could C-

Note really become one of the most popular pop acts in
the world?

If Louis Pearlman thought so, then who were they to
argue?

3

Building a Pop Empire

Behind every great band stands a great manager. C-Note may have had all the makings of pop stardom, but if it wasn't for the generous assistance of one visionary, it may have taken them much longer than four years to step into the spotlight. Groups like the Beatles, the Jackson Five, New Edition, and the Spice Girls all had someone looking out for their best interests; someone who would arrange their flights, their meals, their concert appearances, and even their clothes. For C-Note, that someone was none other than pop impresario Louis J. Pearlman.

An instrumental force behind C-Note's popularity, Pearlman took the boys under his powerful wing and gave them the tools they needed to succeed in the music industry. Whether it was landing them a record contract, choreographing their dances, or getting them on television shows, Pearlman made all the arrangements for C-Note's coming-out party.

When talking about C-Note, it's almost impossible not to pay a tribute to the fascinating and charismatic entrepreneur who made their rise to stardom possible. So without further ado . . .

SETTING THE STAGE

Few people could ever have guessed that the shy, portly young kid from Queens, New York would one day become one of the richest and most powerful men in the music industry. Louis Pearlman's childhood betrayed no signs of his future business prowess. Born in 1954 to a dry cleaner and a milkmaid, Pearlman was a good student, but showed no real affinity for academics.

He was, however, smitten by the showbiz bug.

Pearlman was first exposed to the glamorous life when his cousin, Art Garfunkel, came to fame as one half of the Simon and Garfunkel duo. Responsible for such timeless hits as "Mrs. Robinson" and "The Sounds of Silence," Simon and Garfunkel were America's premier singing/songwriting team. Watching his cousin get all the fame and attention, Pearlman couldn't help but want some of that glory for himself. Since his family had never had very much money, the lure of rock 'n roll's fast cash and freewheeling lifestyle proved too strong to resist.

At sixteen years of age, Pearlman decided to stake his own claim in the music industry by forming a band called Flyer with some high school friends. The group wasn't an immediate success, but soon they were getting gigs in New York City, opening for such musical legends as Kool & the Gang and Barry White. Pearlman loved being on stage and wanted to devote the rest of his life to making music.

Pearlman continued playing with the band even after he began attending Queens College in 1975. But during his junior year, the band broke up, leaving Pearlman baffled as to what he should do with the rest of his life. After playing with the same group of guys for five years, starting a new band didn't seem too appealing. Nevertheless, he needed an auxiliary income to pay for his tuition. That's when he took a part-time job working as a blimp handler at New Jersey's Teterboro Airport.

Pearlman had been fascinated by aircraft from an early age. When he was only ten years old, he'd experienced his first blimp sighting. Watching as the vessel sailed amongst the clouds, the young boy was all rapt attention. Aircraft became his sole interest outside of music. When he took the blimp-handling position, Pearlman figured that it would give him a chance to make some money and pursue his hobby at the same time. He had no idea that working at the airport would bring him face-to-face with the American dream.

Business executives from all over the country would fly in on private jets, and would then be ushered into Manhattan via limousines. That's when Louis was struck by a brilliant idea: Why not cut down on precious moments by flying the execs into the city by helicopter.

Completely enamored with the commuter-helicopter scheme, Pearlman wasted no time in drafting up a business plan in one of his business classes. His instructor was so impressed with the concept that he encouraged Louis to take the idea to the next level. After finding the right investors, Pearlman was fast on his way to becoming a millionaire.

Pretty soon, Pearlman's business expanded to include his favorite of all aircraft—the blimp. He began providing blimps for McDonald's, Budweiser, and Fuji film, and was so successful that he even branched out into chartering planes for such luminaries as Michael Jackson, the Rolling Stones, and other rock icons.

Today, he owns 47 planes and his aviation division boasts an estimated worth of $950 million. Not bad for a kid from Queens.

SUNNY DAYS

Tired of long New York winters, Pearlman migrated to sunny Orlando, Florida, where he could enjoy the fine weather from the comfort of his stately mansion. At first he made use of the local business opportunities by buying a frozen yogurt franchise, a chain of pizzerias, and a travel agency. Life had never been quite so bright as it was in Orlando.

Still, something was missing.

No matter how much capital he amassed, all business ventures paled in comparison to the glitz of the entertainment industry. As they say in show business, there's no business like show business.

For his first foray into the entertainment industry, Louis acquired the Chippendales male dancers franchise. He auditioned the guys and even managed the troupe's daily affairs, arranging everything from publicity stunts to his forte, transportation. But even as he profited a hefty commission for his role as owner, Pearlman continued to be drawn by the siren song of the music industry.

In the early months of 1989, Pearlman got a call asking to lease one of his $250,000-per-month jets. This was nothing out of the ordinary, except that the leasers were none other than the teen sensations of yesteryear, the New Kids on the Block. Pearlman was amazed that kids their age could afford to charter one of his planes. But after consulting with his cousin Art, he discovered that these young boys were some of the richest and most popular performers in the world. "I thought to myself, 'I am on the wrong side of the business,' " he explained to the *Fort Worth Star-Telegram*.

Since New Kids could sell millions of dollars' worth of records and merchandise, Pearlman thought that he, too, could put together a group with similar success. After checking out the New Kids in action during a concert, Pearlman became determined to build his own pop sensation from the ground up. After all, how hard could it be?

Instead of rushing headlong into a business he had no idea about, Pearlman made like a savvy entrepreneur and researched the legendary music mogul Berry Gordy as well as his Motown dynasty. He even went so far as to get counsel from Smokey Robinson, one of the most famous and widely respected Motown artists. From Robinson, he learned everything he knows about fostering a comfortable working atmosphere and soothing rivalry between groups. To this very day, Pearlman still adheres to the artist's words of wisdom. "I never forgot what Smokey told me," Pearlman told the *Los Angeles Times*. "This was my education."

Another important lesson came from studying the New Kids's blueprint for success. Through his research, Louis uncovered a fascinating fact: He found that the majority of their earnings came from licensed merchandise like T-shirts, calendars, and dolls, as opposed to their record sales. Had he not seen the figures with his own two eyes, Louis would never have thought this possible. To capitalize on this most lucrative opportunity, he incorporated a special merchandise division into his newly formed company called Trans Continental Records.

When the New Kids lost steam in 1993, the music industry was reluctant to accept any new boy bands. The auditoriums grew emptier by the day, the merchandise stopped selling, and the fans were weary of the overexposed pop group. According to most industry insiders, the backlash against the New Kids and the bubblegum pop they represented was here to stay. Teens no longer wanted to have anything to do with the lighthearted and upbeat sounds of pop music, and were now exploring the wilder world of grunge rock. Record executives refused even to consider the idea of signing an all-boy band.

It was obvious that anyone wishing to launch a new group would have their work cut out for them.

Despite the numerous naysayers, Pearlman was determined to make his new pop enterprise work. He was convinced that if he found the right group of guys, with good voices, dance steps, and looks to match, they could go just as far as the New Kids on the Block had in their heyday.

Orlando was the perfect location for his new venture. With its balmy weather, endless stream of tourists and concertgoers, amusement parks, and young talent looking to make it big, the city had everything that a fledgling music company needed to take flight.

But before he could begin scouting the area for the ideal combination of young performers, he would have to find a place where they could practice and record. He searched the environs and finally found a vast warehouse where the group of young hopefuls would be transformed into seasoned superstars.

THE FIRST GENERATION

Once he had the time and the place all picked out, Pearlman announced his auditions throughout the city of Orlando. Over sixty young boys showed up to compete for the five slots that were open. All of them had talent, but three guys, namely Nick Carter, Howie Dorough, and A. J. McLean, stood out from the pack. More auditions were held to complete the lineup. That's when Kevin Richardson joined the crew, and brought his cousin Brian Littrell to round out the outfit.

The year was 1993, and the group would be called the Backstreet Boys.

The five guys selected had no idea what fate would await them. All they knew is that they would be paid $500 to $1,000 a week to improve themselves. With dance lessons, vocal training, and a complete image overhaul handed to the quintet on a silver platter, one would have thought that it was the guys of Backstreet who were paying Louis Pearlman. But Louis wouldn't think of taking a dime from the new recruits. He did, however, draft an agreement that allotted him a certain portion of the group's income, if and when they ever made any money.

Pearlman knew that, as with most investments, his latest endeavor came with no guarantees. He could only do so much, and then the public would have to decide the group's fate. Control was a rare commodity in the business, but Pearlman found that he could get more leverage by hiring people who had experience in the pop music business. As the former tour managers for the New Kids, Johnny Wright and his wife Donna were just the people to join the Trans Con family as the Backstreet Boys' comanagers. They had the skills, the know-how, and the experience that would give the boys an edge in the marketplace.

Pearlman ran a very tight ship. He took control of every aspect of the boys' careers, including their look, their music, and their dance moves. Because he was investing thousands upon thousands of his hard-earned dollars in this venture, he wasn't about to risk losing it all. The Backstreet Boys welcomed his input and respected their fearless leader. Pretty soon, the group and Pearlman became one big happy family.

When the boys were finally ready to take their act to the streets, they began by playing small gigs at restaurants and shopping malls. But their first large venue performance didn't happen until May 1993, at Sea World. The boys gave the show everything they had, but the response of the crowd was lukewarm at best. The audience was just not ready to embrace pop music.

Not to be deterred by the public's response, Pearlman had the boys record a demo, which he took to record label executives around the country. Unfortunately they, too, weren't ready for the Backstreet Boys. Pearlman was saddened by the news. He had worked so hard to give the boys a start in the business, and worried that he wouldn't be able to make good on his promise. "It was hard. Lou shopped the group to ten different labels and nobody was interested," Alan Siegal, the current manager of C-Note, told the *Los Angeles Times*. "Everybody said the so-called boy band thing is over. Nobody knew these guys or wanted to."

Hiring Johnny Wright proved to be one of the smartest ideas Pearlman had ever had. Wright was the one who finally suggested that the Backstreet Boys explore the European music market. East of the Atlantic, alternative rock had not become the monopoly that it had in the States, and the Backstreet Boys stood a much better chance of launching their career overseas.

True to the Wright's word, the Backstreet Boys were an instant hit with German fans. "We were right," Wright explained. "They exploded." The group was selling out huge auditoriums, and after two years had sold over eight million records.

Their new record label, Jive, was quick to jump on the bandwagon. If Backstreet could incite European fans to riot and storm the stage, they just might have the stuff to bring American audiences to their knees as well. In 1997, after two years of nonstop touring in Europe, the musical expatriates were reintroduced to their homeland. This time, the Backstreet Boys would not have to work so hard. Millions of fans came out to greet the boys' arrival and invest their hard-earned baby-sitting incomes and allowances into the group's debut album.

Meanwhile, Louis Pearlman was becoming increasingly more confident about his prospects in the music biz. He was so proud of his first group's success that he decided to start another group. Instead of being complacent and bragging about his accomplishment, Pearlman wanted to prove to the critics that the Backstreet Boys' triumphant spree in Europe and the United States was not just a fluke. Of course, the idea of making even more money was also a consideration. As he told the *Los Angeles Times*, "You can't make money on an airline with just one airplane."

Pearlman wanted to create another group that would be just as popular as the Backstreet Boys. By now, word of the famous Louis Pearlman had gotten around the streets of Orlando. Every up-and-coming young singer wanted to become a part of the Trans Con family. So when Pearlman announced another round of auditions, hundreds of young men came out of the woodwork. Watching all the boys file into his pop music complex, Pearlman was pleased to find that his reputation had preceded him.

But with so many new faces to choose from, Louis found that selecting a new group would prove even more difficult than before. It seemed that the guys were even more competitive and talented this time around. After the last dance routine was completed and the final note sung, Pearlman and his support network of choreographers, producers, and stylists finally had a meeting of the minds. After deliberating for what seemed like hours, five young aspirants were picked to join the group that would later be called 'N Sync.

Justin Timberlake, Chris Kirkpatrick, Joey Fatone, Lance Bass, and JC Chasez were the answer to every girl's dream. After taking them through the same performance boot camp that the Backstreet Boys had gone through, Louis shipped them off to Germany, where three of their singles were quickly catapulted into that country's Top Ten.

By 1999, the Backstreet Boys had grossed more than $900 million in record, video, and merchandise sales. With a Grammy nomination for Best New Artist, countless magazine articles, and web shrines to their greatness, the Backstreet Boys proved to be a powerful force in the music industry.

'N Sync had, by this time, returned to the States a bona fide overseas success story. Duly blessed with charisma, attitude, and good looks, Pearlman's newest quintet posed a threat to the Backstreet Boys' popularity, and the latter group decided to leave Pearlman and seek representation elsewhere.

Sure enough, 'N Sync and the Backstreet Boys were soon running neck and neck in the popularity polls. The two boy bands became rivals for the top slots on MTV's *Total Request Live* and the Billboard Top Forty. "They are just huge with our viewers," Tom Calderon, an MTV exec, told the *Los Angeles Times*. "And the thing that is most amazing is the incredible passion of the fans. They can't get enough."

THE POP REVIVAL

Whether you think Pearlman is a revolutionary genius or not, there's still something to be said for being in the right place at the right time. He had predicted one of the strongest pop revolutions of our time, and if that doesn't make him a latter-day Nostradamus, what does?

From 1992 to 1996, pop music had gone the way of the dinosaurs. It was as if the New Kids, Debbie Gibson, and Tiffany had never existed at all. Blame it on the edgy alternative rock sound or the pulsating beats of hip-hop. Whatever the explanation, young kids didn't want to have anything to do with pop music.

Today, the days of gloom, doom, and all-consuming angst seem like ancient history to all but the most stalwart Korn fans. Back in 1993, however, groups like Nirvana and Pearl Jam were tearing up the music charts and pushing the likes of C-Note, Backstreet Boys, and Hanson off to the sidelines. "For a while there, kids wanted to be older than they were," David Zedeck, owner of Renaissance Entertainment in New York City, told *Time* magazine. "Now kids want to be kids again. It's the effect of Disney and Nickelodeon on the music industry."

In January 1997, some three years after Kurt Cobain's suicide and amidst the continued rivalries within the hip-hop community, a group of sassy, young British girls stormed into America.

They called themselves the Spice Girls, and the country has yet to recover from their invasion.

With their message of "girl power" and their brazen

attitudes and outfits, the girls were like fresh air in a stale musical climate. The country went mad for the five exports, and began buying up their album with all the vigor of the group's high-energy dance numbers. The pop rock outing of the brothers Hanson enjoyed similar success. Soon other groups followed. First the Backstreet Boys; then 'N Sync and 98°. And last but not least, our very own C-Note.

With the economy doing so well, kids had more money to spend than ever before, and no one understood the full impact of this upward economic cycle better than Pearlman. "When girls scream and ask for CDs and posters, are their daddies going to say no? I don't think so," Pearlman explained. "It works nice for us."

Like it or not—and if you're reading this book, chances are you do—the country has pop on the brain. And with the success of such artists as C-Note, Backstreet Boys, Hanson, and Britney Spears, it looks like pop music is here for the long haul.

ALL IN THE FAMILY

Even though Pearlman is as shrewd a businessman as they come, he is also one of the kindest and most giving men in the industry. Just looking around the Trans Con facility, it becomes very clear that the proprietor's main priority is keeping his musical family happy.

With video games, bright posters, and a cozy rec room, the Trans Con warehouse has come to resemble a full-amenities summer camp more than a boot camp. It is a place where all of the Trans Con groups, the latest of which are C-Note, Innosence, Take 5, and Lyte Funkie Ones (LFO), can gather and take a break from the rigors of their daily training sessions.

The Trans Con warehouse functions like a well-oiled machine. Pearlman never spares any expense to provide his groups with the best choreographers, stylists, and personal trainers money can buy. It's no wonder why all of the Trans Con family members have such a profound respect and appreciation for their mentor.

Going by the example of their magnanimous benefactor, members from various groups have managed to form deep friendships with one another. Rivalries of any kind are discouraged at Trans Con. Instead, an atmosphere of encouragement pervades the facility where C-Note has been training for the past three years. The members of the Trans Con family couldn't be prouder of one another's triumphs, and never miss an opportunity to display their affection. "It took me a few weeks to get used to everyone hugging each other in the halls," Jay Marose, a Trans Con exec, explained.

One thing you could say about Pearlman is that he is always there for his artists. Whether they need a hug, a nice word, or extra money, he is only too willing to oblige. It's no wonder his merry clan has taken to calling him "Big Poppa." Every word he says and everything he does for his groups shows them just how much he cares about seeing them rise to stardom.

Getting to the top is one thing, but Pearlman never loses sight of the fact that his groups need even more support when they are still unknowns. Because some of the guys have problems making ends meet in the beginning of their careers, Louis provides them with a substantial salary that comes right out of his own pocket. On occasion, he has also gone so far as to help out the groups' families when they are in need. Ask anyone who works with him, and they'll tell you that he is one of the most generous men in the business.

Since Trans Con is all about creating a family atmosphere, Pearlman never forgets that his young guys and girls have families who miss them back home. Many of his musical prodigies are not Orlando natives, and have to endure long separations from their loved ones. Unwilling to see his troops struggle with bouts of homesickness, Pearlman makes a concerted effort to reunite the families. He has even gone so far as to stage elab-

C-Note serenades the crowd at a packed New York City appearance.

Raul shares his passion with the fans.

Photo by Janine Davic

Dru flashes that killer smile that drives girls crazy!

Photo by Janine Davic

Raul and Brody strike a pose while promoting *A Different Kind of Love.*

Photo by Janine Davic

David shines as he flashes his pearly whites.

Photo by Janine Davic

Raul, Dru, and David work the audience with their gorgeous harmonies . . .

Photo by Janine Davic

. . . and their slammin' dance moves.

Photo by Janine Davic

At an in-store appearance, Dru lets the song come from his heart.

Photo by Janine Davic

D'Lo shows off some of his best assets: his sultry voice
and those sexy muscles!

Photo by Janine Davic

C-Note's heading straight to the top!

orate parties in New York City (which include flying all of the group's family members on his own aircraft) and throwing fun pool parties in Orlando.

Through it all—the struggles and the triumphs— Pearlman never loses sight of the real reason he has gotten involved in show business in the first place. From day one, he strove to create something special and totally unique, an environment that would foster artistic growth and creativity. And with Trans Continental Records, that's precisely what he has managed to do. "Backstreet Boys look at me as the sixth Backstreet Boy," he once conveyed to MTV. " 'N Sync also looks at me as like the Big Poppa. I think that they all know that what I've done is from sincerity, is from the heart. It's been developing a family."

TAKING CARE OF C-NOTE

Pearlman may be famous for lavishing special attention on his roster of young performers, but when it comes to C-Note he is known for going above and beyond the call of duty. Since their first day on the job, Raul, Brody, David, and Dru have permanently enjoyed Pearlman's good graces. Noticing that they were tapping into the lucrative Latin market, Pearlman saw the potential long before Ricky Martin and Jennifer Lopez became mainstream hits.

When the group first came to him, he loved their style and energy. But that didn't mean that they could just kick back, relax, and watch the fans multiply. On the contrary, it was their terrific potential for fame and fortune that had Pearlman paying special attention to their progress and pushing them to be their very best.

He has gotten so involved in the guys' careers that they often playfully poke fun at him for being overprotective. As he had with Backstreet Boys and 'N Sync before them, Pearlman watches over every facet of C-Note's career, from their clothes to their videos to their song titles. There are no lengths to which he will not go to make sure that the group attains the success that is rightfully theirs. "C-Note is going to be huge," Pearlman asserted to the *Los Angeles Times*. "No doubt."

Many people would think that by now Pearlman is just too busy and too powerful to take an active interest in his groups. Nothing could be further from the truth. In fact, the more goals he achieves, the more he sets. Pearlman is so involved with C-Note that he makes sure to attend all of their training sessions and concerts. If the boys happened to be booked to sing at a festival, a restaurant, or even a local park, Pearlman is bound to be there cheering them on. He gets so excited about seeing the group perform, you'd think that he was their very own cheering section. Always beaming with pride and respect for the guys' hard work and dedication, Louis Pearlman is much like a devoted father who never misses his son's Little League game.

4

Basic Training

C-Note's career couldn't have been going any better had the guys planned it themselves. Even now, they are quick to say that joining forces with Louis Pearlman was the best thing that had ever happened to them. At last they would have the chance to hone their skills and prepare themselves to conquer the world of pop music.

But once the papers had been signed and C-Note had been officially welcomed into the Trans Con family, the boys realized just how much work still lay ahead of them. While Pearlman's industry connections would get their feet in the door, the guys would have to do some fancy footwork if they wanted to keep that door from slamming shut.

Fortunately, the C-Note crew was more than willing to break a sweat. There wasn't anything they wouldn't do to get their music heard by as many people as possible. And if that meant suffering through twenty-hour workdays and putting their social lives on indefinite hold, it was a compromise they were willing to make.

A COMMITMENT TO EXCELLENCE

Few fans know how much work goes into the making of a pop supergroup. Months—sometimes years—of sleepless nights, dance rehearsals, vocal training, and recording have to be completed before a group can make their grand entrance into the world at large. Anyone can fall in love with a group once their harmonies are polished and their stage moves are perfectly synchronized, but it is only the die-hard fanatics who can truly appreciate all of the steps that a group needs to take before unveiling their act for the first time.

Unless you were there to see the transformation, C-Note's journey from anonymity to stardom would normally be off-limits. That's because few groups want you to see all the hard work they have to endure. But now, with our help, fans can get a rare bird's-eye view into the making of C-Note, from its first days at Trans Con to its first large-venue debut.

When David, Raul, Brody, and Dru first arrived on the scene, they were like hatchlings struggling to find their legs. Although they had worked out their own repertoire, everything they had learned prior to signing with Trans Con would have to be forgotten. If Pearlman was to succeed in re-creating the magic he had worked for the Backstreet Boys and 'N Sync, he and the guys would have to start from scratch.

Of course, it didn't hurt that the foursome had innate talent. Without their superior vocal and dance skills, Louis would have had nothing to work with. But since the guys of C-Note worked so hard prior to coming on board, their aptitude for the ins and outs of show biz surprised even their mentor.

Nestled deep within Orlando's industrial district, the Trans Con compound was to be C-Note's home for several years. At first sight, the boys thought the building looked like a giant factory. But once they got inside and had the chance to check out all the gold and platinum plaques lining the walls, as well as the countless posters of their predecessors, 'N Sync and Backstreet Boys, they were thrilled to be part of the team.

Soon, Raul, David, Dru, and Brody were introduced to all the other groups, as well as to their own personal coaches. C-Note was instantly won over by everyone they encountered. People they had just met were hugging them and praising their talents. The whole experience made them feel like they'd died and gone to musical heaven. "The whole Trans Con family is pretty, you know, it's a pretty tight-knit circle," Dru told MTV. "I mean, we have so many bands, from Backstreet, we got 'N Sync, LFO, Innosence, and then of course, us."

At first, Pearlman let the guys of C-Note wander about and explore their new surroundings. He watched on happily as the new recruits ingratiated themselves into the hearts of his staff members. But once the guys had finally learned the lay of the land, Pearlman sat down with them and outlined the program that they would have to follow. "We have like a little boot camp down in Orlando and what we do is we have choreographers," he said. "We have vocal coaches. We have a recording studio and so forth."

That's when the C-Note guys realized just how much effort they would have to put forth. From dawn till dusk for many months to come, the group would be engaged in what amounted to a comprehensive crash course in pop stardom. Pearlman had thought of everything, and didn't leave one hour of their day unaccounted for. During the meeting, Raul, David, Brody, and Dru made a commitment to becoming the best. In turn, Louis Pearlman promised the guys that he would give them no less than his 100 percent, as long as they stayed dedicated and never lost sight of the final goal.

Whether it was singing lessons or working out at the gym, the schedule was predetermined to guarantee that C-Note would reach its full potential. "This system is a dream for anybody who wants to do this for a living,"

Raul explained to Gavin.com. "They do everything they can to let you develop as an artist. Louis knew what he wanted; he knew how he wanted to set it up . . . like a new version of what Berry Gordy did at Motown."

From the time they first arrived, Raul, David, Brody, and Dru were overjoyed by the rigorous schedule. To them it seemed that the more they worked, the more successful they would become. It was this positive mental attitude that helped them achieve their goals one day at a time.

Before they knew it, the guys of C-Note had become such a well-functioning team that they barely even recognized themselves.

So gung ho were they about perfecting themselves that their instructors actually began to fear for their well-being. No one wanted the C-Notes to overexert themselves and burn out. So instead of listening to their coaches' pep talks, it was Raul, David, Brody, and Dru who were encouraging the experts to push even harder. For these guys, there was never such a thing as a middle ground or coming in second best. Either C-Note was going to become the best pop group in music history or the members would die trying.

PUTTING IT ALL TOGETHER

If you had asked any of the guys from C-Note about what goes into the making of a major pop star before their Trans Con days, they would have told you that it pretty much all comes down to singing, dancing, and good fortune. Little did they know how much is actually involved in launching a pop act.

Part of their daily responsibilities included something called media training. When fans see the guys being interviewed by reporters and talk show hosts, they usually marvel at the ease with which they handle themselves. What many onlookers don't know is that it took years for Raul, Dru, David, and Brody to become so comfortable in front of the camera.

With the help of their instructor, Jay Marose, the C-Notes learned how to handle themselves in any media-related situation. Whether they were going to be interviewed on a television show, for a magazine, or at a press conference, Raul, Brody, David, and Dru would have to learn the basic tricks of the trade. They would have to study how to make eye contact with the reporters, interact with one another on screen, and keep the audience interested.

To that end, their instructor and public relations VP at Trans Continental Records, Jay Marose, videotaped the boys during mock interview sessions. He would then play back the tapes and point out what the guys had done wrong or praise them when they incorporated his corrections. Watching themselves acting all serious on videotape, Raul, Brody, David, and Dru could never resist poking fun at each other. In the end, it turned out to be one of the most enjoyable classes in their pop academy curriculum. "Media training is . . . what we'll do is we'll go in the office and we'll meet with our media director, his name is Jay Marose," Dru elaborated to MTV. "And he'll sit us down and kind of prepares you for different kinds of questions. And, you know, how to answer them. You know, your mannerisms, like not putting your hand in front of your mouth, and all that kind of stuff."

At first, the guys had trouble keeping their composure during the mock interviews. They would break out laughing in the middle of an answer or start fidgeting with their clothes, hair, or pencils. The problem was, they were just too excited for their own good. However, by the time they were actually giving interviews for national magazines and newspapers, they were as professional and polished as news broadcasters. "Actually, most of that training was to prepare us to be on-camera," Raul confided to Gavin.com. "You know, stuff like not scraping your chair during an interview, maintaining eye contact, not putting your hand in front of your face, and not picking your nose."

While they were learning to talk the talk, the guys were also being groomed for success. If they were going to be larger than life, their image, clothes, and overall presentation would need some serious fine-tuning.

Although each C-Note was blessed with natural good looks, it was up to Pearlman and his team to accentuate the positive and downplay the negative. Everything from the way the guys held their microphones to the way they smiled for the cameras would be up for serious evaluation. As Alan Sicgal, C-Note's manager, explained to MTV, "We'll be looking to have a definitive style and image to differentiate C-Note from other acts that might be out there. And hone in on each particular guy's best features and create a final image that we'll be presenting to the public."

Even as he was bringing in one top image consultant after another, Pearlman would ask the boys to participate in the decision-making process and offer their feedback. The last thing Pearlman wanted was for Raul, David, Brody, and Dru to be uncomfortable with their appearance. After all, each group member had a very distinct personality, and part of style management is to bring out each individual's unique appeal.

Once all the measurements had been taken and the trendsetters consulted, C-Note had undergone a major makeover. Now the guys not only conducted themselves like stars but looked the part as well.

All flash and no substance, however, would not do for this gifted quartet. They wanted to have the skills to back up their good looks and winning smiles. So while they were busy sweating to the oldies with their personal trainer and carving out what is now their signature C-Note look, Raul, David, Brody, and Dru undertook an exacting vocal training regime.

Initially, the guys had thought that their vocals would be the one thing that they wouldn't have to work on.

But when they combined singing with the vigorous dance combinations conceived by their choreographer, they realized that there was a lot of work that still needed to be done. "We came in and we started singing and dancing and the next thing you know, we were like huffing and puffing," David reported to MTV. "Working with the vocal coach, he helps us out with that as far as our breathing goes."

The one thing that the guys didn't have any trouble with was their dancing. Outside of learning how to manage their cumbersome microphones, Raul, David, Dru, and Brody were expert dancers. Their many trips to the local nightclubs had paid off. Once they had committed the dance routines to memory, they had no trouble executing the complex and often strenuous moves required by their dance numbers. Much to the choreographer's surprise, David, who is one of the best dancers in the group, was instrumental in adding some of the more street-savvy choreography to the routines.

No matter how much the group exerted themselves, their motivation never wavered. They knew how fortunate they were to be given the chance to better themselves, and are still feeling indebted to Pearlman for teaching them the business. "Dancing came with the singing," Raul told MTV. "Then rehearsing, then learning how to use the mike. You know, not getting the mike, not swallowing it. Those are all techniques that people don't know that they need to use. And those are all things that because we have facilities at our disposal, we were able to learn."

WHAT'S IN A NAME

If you have been paying attention, you probably noticed that we have been calling the group "C-Note" from the beginning of this story. But the band would not officially be called C-Note until the guys arrived at Trans Continental Records. Before then, the group had gone through a variety of names. But Pearlman didn't like any of them, and left it up to the guys to find a new name that would accurately convey their attitudes, musical style, and beliefs to their fans.

Choosing a name is a veritable rite of passage for any group. A good name can speak volumes about the group, while a misnomer can detract from the overall image to disastrous effect. The guys of C-Note knew that this was a matter they couldn't take lightly. Whatever name they chose, they would have to live with it for the rest of their careers. Pressured to come up with the goods, Raul, Brody, David, and Dru became anxious about finding the perfect moniker for the group.

After sitting down to brainstorm on countless occasions, the boys found that they were stumped. The pressure had gotten to them, and try as they might, they simply couldn't come up with a handle that truly encompassed who they were. For all their trouble, the guys were no better off than when they started. Actually, they were more confused than ever.

Seeking counsel from the experienced Pearlman also didn't help. Their leader, as it turned out, was determined that the group should choose a name on their own. The desire to foster independence and self-reliance in the guys led him to take a hands-off approach in the name department. And while he would have final approval once Raul, Brody, David, and Dru had chosen a title, he would not interfere until they had come up with something on their own.

Taking a cue from their wise counselor, the guys renewed their commitment to finding the perfect name. They also realized that by putting too much pressure on themselves, they were developing what is known as a "creative block." To alleviate this all-too-common malady, Brody, David, Dru, and Raul decided to give themselves a break. Since the hand of inspiration would not be forced, they took a break from the name game until they were in a more relaxed state of mind.

One day, when the guys were taking a breather from their pop studies, they were deeply engrossed in a football game on TV. With empty pizza boxes littering the floor and all the guys reclining on their plush couches, it became clear that this was as relaxed as they were ever going to get. It was the perfect time to brainstorm a new name for the group.

With pen and paper in hand, Dru told the guys to call out group names at random, at which point he would write them down on a piece of paper. Some of the names were actually quite good, while others were mediocre. As the guys looked over the fruits of their labor and tried to select the top contenders, Dru had a epiphany. "And it just popped in my head," Dru revealed during *Soul Train*. "I was like, 'How about C-Note?' And they were like, 'Yeah, sure!' And we were thinking, like what does it mean. It means like a 100-dollar bill, it means mint, it means, you know, 100 percent."

"C-Note" was an instant hit with all of the guys. It was the first name on which all of them could agree. The reason they liked it so much is that it was catchy and easy to remember. It was also a name that said exactly what kind of performers they wanted to be.

After playing around with the various meanings and implications of their new label, the guys realized that the C-Note tag could also double as their own personal motto. For as long as they could remember, they had been striving to achieve excellence in their music, presentation, and attitudes. Now was their chance to share this all-encompassing goal with the rest of the world. "Then we put our own little thing to it," Dru explained. "Let's Create Nothing Other Than Excellence, which means that we never settle for anything we've ever done. So that we always take it to the next level and get better and better."

Raul, Brody, Dru, and David couldn't believe that they had come up with such a perfect name on their own. This triumph was one of their first, and they wanted to share the moment with Pearlman. As soon as they had the busy man's attention, they blurted out the name and waited in anticipation as he considered the prospect. After spending a couple of minutes in deep thought, Pearlman looked up and smiled as if to say, "You've got yourself a name!"

From that point on, the group would always be known as C-Note.

THE BIG DEBUT

With a name to call their own and years of rehearsal and practice behind them, the guys of C-Note were beginning to get antsy about performing in front of a crowd. Having labored so diligently for so long, the guys were finally starting to lose their patience. They were almost bursting at the seams trying to get Pearlman to agree to let them perform. If they failed, they would do better next time. If they succeeded, they would have the confidence to repeat the performance.

Of course, finding the perfect event to showcase C-Note's newly acquired chops would be no easy task. Pearlman had to be very careful. If the show was too large, the boys might have come down with an egregious case of stage fright. Yet, should the venue prove too small, they would fail to get the exposure they needed to become successful.

But when it came to wrangling the horns of a dilemma, Perlman was never at a loss for long. For the past several months, he had been busy orchestrating a live event called "Orlando Bands Together." The show was actually a fund-raiser for tornado relief, and featured a show-stopping lineup that included the Backstreet Boys, Vanilla Ice, and 'N Sync.

Originally, Louis hadn't planned on unveiling C-Note at the show, but the more he thought about it, the more the idea appealed to him. Even though the show was going to be huge, attracting every teen in the Orlando area, the guys of C-Note had come a long way. And after watching them run through the routines with all the expertise of seasoned professionals, Pearlman decided that they were ready to take on the challenge. On March 3, 1998, Raul, Brody, Dru, and David would graduate to the big time.

No one was more pleased with the news than C-Note. They were so happy with the arrangement that they started cheering and hugging Louis. That night, the boys even scheduled a mini celebration to commemorate their arrival.

Slowly but surely, their excitement was replaced with a healthy dose of nervous tension. They had been so anxious to strut their stuff in front of a crowd, that they lost sight of the fact that this would be their first performance at a large concert. But the nervous tension didn't last long—eventually it gave way to a full-blown panic attack.

Hearing the details of the concert also didn't help matters much. Not only was the turnout expected to exceed ten thousand people, but the show was scheduled to be broadcast live over the Internet, where hundreds of thousands of people could watch them perform. Further exacerbating their fear was the fact that they would have to perform alongside two of the world's most popular pop groups. After seeing dozens of posters of the Backstreet Boys and 'N Sync all over the Trans Con building, Raul, David, Brody, and Dru were in awe of the success of these groups. The chance to warm up the crowds for their role models was just too much to handle.

Seeing that the guys needed a major confidence boost, Pearlman took them aside and tried to alleviate their worries. He spoke of the old days, when the Backstreet Boys had just started in the business. Much like C-Note, they, too, had been nervous about getting on stage, but look at them now. Louis's consideration for the guys' feelings was always apparent. Even though he had given them so much in terms of financial support, the right connections, and a full training course, nothing was as valuable as the encouragement he gave them at this crucial juncture in their careers.

When the fateful date arrived, the guys of C-Note were still in the throes of panic. Short of hypnosis, they had tried everything to combat their ever-growing anxiety—breathing exercises, yoga, playing sports, you name it. Nothing worked. Resigned to their state of perpetual worry, Brody, Dru, David, and Raul arrived on the scene prepared to face the music. The anxiety had turned into a bundle of energy, and it seemed as if they just wanted to get the whole thing over with so they could get a decent night's sleep.

After being groomed by the stylists and donning their matching wardrobes, the guys were ready to go on. But first they would have to scan the scene from the comfort of the backstage area. Much to their surprise, seeing thousands of smiling faces didn't scare them as much as they thought it would. In fact, they actually became excited about singing in front of the crowd. A final pep talk from Pearlman, and the boys were ready to make their move.

As soon as they sang their first song, they knew they were a hit. The fans' cheers, screams, and happy faces combined to form something akin to a welcome wagon, making the quartet feel loved and wanted. Raul, Brody, David, and Dru couldn't believe how well they were being received. The guys were also surprised by the high caliber of their own performance. It was as if the support of the audience was giving them the strength to overcome their fears and put on a heated and energetic show.

Midway through their set, girls began crying and throwing their phone numbers and belongings on the stage. They simply couldn't get enough of the guys. In all fairness, C-Note's stage presence was unbelievable. The guys executed their steps with perfect grace and precision, and their voices never sounded better. With every song, it seemed as if the group was developing more and more confidence. After bringing thousands of girls to their knees with the songs "So Often," "My Heart Belongs to You," and "Wait Till I Get Home," Raul, David, Brody, and Dru left the stage in a state of euphoria. They were so dazed by what had transpired in those brief, make-it or break-it moments that they could barely hear the clamor of thousands of people applauding.

When they were finally within the safe confines of the backstage, they were greeted by all of the Trans Con family, including Louis and the members of Backstreet Boys and 'N Sync. Feeling dazed and confused, the guys of C-Note actually had to be told that they'd been a smash hit. And with so many people praising their big debut, there was no doubt in their minds that they had indeed caused quite a stir.

Tired and panting from their long set, Raul, David, Brody, and Dru thought they were done for the day. But the fun had just begun. Apparently, someone at the Trans Con offices had arranged for the guys to do a live chat with three thousand of their newest fans from the Internet community. This was also something totally new to the guys. It was as if they were getting a crash course in public exposure. First singing in front of ten thousand people; and then talking with three thousand audience members.

For a lesser group, this sudden burst of activity might have been too much to deal with, but C-Note was ready for anything. Once the fans started firing off questions, the guys were quick to respond with all the humor and intelligence they could muster their first time out. The fans loved it.

But all good things must come to an end, and C-Note's first online chat would soon be history. Much to their new fans' disappointment, when the other groups had finished their sets and the concert was officially over, the guys had to run along. A small crowd had formed, waiting to congratulate them on a job well done.

5

Just Rewards

C-Note's victorious debut in Orlando was nothing short of miraculous. Not only did they hold their own beside veteran pop acts; they proved to themselves that there was nothing they couldn't do. For a pop group waiting to break into the mainstream, this type of boundless enthusiasm was just what the doctor ordered.

No one was more excited about the group's admirable entrance into the world of pop rock than Lou Pearlman. He had taken a huge risk letting the guys perform that day, and it had paid off in a big way. How big, exactly? Well, that's something C-Note and Pearlman were about to find out.

AN EPIC EVENT

Once the commotion surrounding their first show had died down, Raul, David, Brody, and Dru were whisked off to the star-studded Trans Con family reunion. The guys, along with all of the coaches and instructors who'd played a hand in their triumph, celebrated the first leg of the group's journey to pop stardom.

The four C-Notes were all emotions and raw nerves.

Now that they had scored big in their first show, they were excited to get back on stage again. They would never forget the rush of seeing thousands of fans grooving to their rhythms, and they wanted to return to the spotlight as soon as possible.

Since the group's debut exceeded everyone's wildest expectations, Pearlman told the guys that from now on they would be regulars on the local music scene. Having shown grace under pressure and courage under a baptism by fire, the guys had proven once and for all that they could handle the responsibility of performing.

Knowing that they had contributed to the worthy cause of tornado relief by making thousands of fans smile, and that they had earned Pearlman's respect, was more than enough of a reward for the guys. They couldn't think of one thing that could make them happier—until Louis came back with a surprise announcement that made their hearts beat even faster.

Apparently, executives from Epic Records had called to congratulate the guys. They had seen them perform during the live web broadcast, and liked what they saw. In fact, the label was so impressed with Pearlman's latest discovery that they invited the guys to perform their own private showcase at Epic headquarters.

Pearlman could barely contain his enthusiasm. He had never expected for the record companies to come calling so soon. The most he had hoped for was to begin spreading news of the group by word of mouth throughout Orlando. Then, and only then, did he think that the group would have the chance to land a contract from a record label. But this was an unprecedented feat. C-Note had only performed in one large show and they were already being wooed by one of the largest and most prestigious labels in the country.

Upon hearing the good word, David, Brody, Dru, and Raul looked at Pearlman as if he had just gone stark, raving mad. How could they, a new group without any track record, have been invited to sing for Epic executives? Either their benevolent leader was playing a cruel joke on them or he hadn't heard the people on the phone correctly.

But Pearlman insisted that he wasn't kidding. After all, C-Note had never been a laughing matter to the businessman. He had believed in them all along.

Once the news of their audition had registered, the guys of C-Note were too pleased for words. They had been so overwhelmed by the day's turn of events, that hearing this amazing news flash sent them straight into the delirium of euphoria. The guys hadn't so much as finished celebrating their first show, and they were already being called back into the Trans Con studios for a full briefing about their meeting with Epic executives.

There was no time to spare. Epic wanted to see them the very next day.

Once again, panic became the group's greatest enemy. All of a sudden, they had a million excuses: they weren't ready . . . what about the plane tickets? How would they act once they got there? What would they wear? In a flurry of mad activity, the Trans Con team readied the guys for their big sendoff. Hotels were booked, clothes were selected, and flights were arranged. All the C-Notes had to do was show up at the office and do what they did best—knock their socks off.

Of course, according to the guys that was all easier said than done. Everything was moving much too fast. They had practiced for years and had had to apply all they'd learned in the span of a few days. From singing in front of a jam-packed crowd to flying to meet with important record executives, this was truly crunch time. Despite the hectic pace, the guys knew that their endurance and strength was being tested. It was a sink-or-swim situation, and they had no intention of going under.

With all of the arrangements made, Raul, Brody, David, and Dru felt like real-life celebrities. Boarding the plane to get to their audition, they couldn't help but feel as if they were flying away into a land of opportunity. Throughout the flight, the guys talked about everything they had gone through, from their earliest years in musical groups to this latest event. They simply couldn't believe how much they had accomplished in such a short period of time.

The next day the boys arrived at Epic Records and were greeted by a group of executives. After engaging in some small talk, the boys were brought into a large room to do their thing. This was a *Flashdance* moment if there ever was one. Picture the edgy and hip guys of C-Note performing in front of a group of buttoned-up, conservative business types. Now that's something we would have all paid to see.

But just like in that eighties film, Raul, Brody, David, and Dru melted the serious facades of the onlookers. By the time they had finished, the executives were clapping for the guys. No one could resist stomping their feet to the catchy rhythm of C-Note's music.

In a private record label showcase such as this, it is customary to wait weeks for the final verdict. Executives usually take their time, researching the group and talking to their management. The guys of C-Note assumed their case would be no exception and went on their merry way.

That night, Brody, Raul, David, and Dru had a long conference about the quality of their performance. In their opinion, they had lived up to their potential. But who knew what was happening behind closed doors. Even though the record label staff appeared to have enjoyed their music, the vote could go either way.

The next day the group returned to their home in Orlando. Their first order of business was to recount all the particulars of their voyage to Pearlman. Once he received the scoop about the executives' foot-stomping reaction, Lou told the guys that they had nothing to worry about. He had been in the business long enough to know when success is imminent, and told the boys that they would have to be patient while Epic outlined all the details.

Trusting their mentor during times of uncertainty had become second nature for the group, but this was an extenuating circumstance. Without a record contract, musical groups can never hope to reach a wide audience. There was just too much riding on Epic's decision. Despite Pearlman's assurances, the guys just couldn't bring themselves to rest easy.

Settling in for what they thought would be an inordinately long waiting period, the guys prepared themselves for the many sleepless nights they would have to endure before learning of the label's verdict. But as soon as Pearlman retired to his office, he received a phone call telling him that Epic had indeed decided to sign C-Note as their newest act.

In all his years in show business, Pearlman had never seen anything like this. The call had come so soon that it had taken him by surprise. Still, there was no way of breaking this type of news gently. Strolling casually into a room where Dru, Brody, David, and Raul were warming up, he quickly blurted out that they had been selected to join such esteemed artists as Jennifer Lopez and B*Witched on Epic's roster of musical acts. Needless to say, all four C-Notes stopped what they were doing and just stared at Pearlman. Had they heard right? Was Pearlman actually telling them that they'd accomplished the unthinkable in just three short days?

As you can guess, the scene in the small rehearsal room was one of utter jubilation. Everyone began hugging each other and praising the Lord. Some of the guys were laughing and others were crying. People started filing into the small rehearsal space to see what all the hubbub was about. While the Trans Con staff could hardly believe that the guys had nabbed a record deal so quickly, all knew that it was well deserved. As one of the most emotionally charged moments of their lives, the memory of that special day would stay with C-Note forever.

Louis Pearlman and his team had come to think of the boys as part of the family, and were extremely proud of their achievements. As Frank Sicolo, vice president of Trans Con, told MTV, "They've really come up through the ranks and they've developed to the point where they are now signed to a major record label, Epic records, which is fantastic."

From virtual unknowns to an overnight success story in less than a week . . . now this *was* too much for them to handle. Even today, long after the initial glee has wore off, the guys get tongue-tied whenever they are asked to describe the events that led up to the biggest triumph of their young lives. "Well, we did a little concert down in Orlando, Orlando Bands Together," Brody recounted the experience on *Soul Train*. "There was a benefit for tornado relief. And they had seen us on the Internet. It was broadcast live over the Internet. And they set up a showcase. So the next day, we flew up there, we did a showcase for them, and we flew back home the next day, and they picked us up that day. That was pretty cool."

Trying to keep their composure in front of a televised audience was probably wise, but when they first heard the news, the last thing on their mind was playing it cool.

IN THE STUDIO WITH C-NOTE

Having had so many dreams come true in such a brief period of time, Raul, Brody, David, and Dru were on top of the world. Their parents were also fiercely proud of their sons. Who would have thought that this music thing would actually pan out?

Once the contractual details had been ironed out and the group had a recording contract to show for themselves, they were apprehensive about what would follow. The obvious next step was to record an album. But they had never before attempted to undertake this formidable challenge. Before joining Trans Con, the group could barely afford to eat, let alone rent out a recording studio and hire producers. They had no idea what went into making an album, and worried about living up to their end of the bargain.

It wasn't every day that a label like Epic came calling, but a contract in itself was no guarantee of success. Experienced or not, the guys would have to step up to the plate and play with the big boys.

Fortunately, Pearlman had been through the recording ringer enough times to have gotten it down to a science. He instructed the guys not to worry themselves needlessly about the process. They had plenty of time to collect new material and polish the album. The most important factor to keep in mind was that the guys should be 100 percent satisfied with their debut effort.

When recording began in the month of July 1998, the quartet was excited about entering the studio. Before they even stepped into the studio, the group was informed that they would be working with some of the industry's leading producers, including Dakari, Guy Roche, Full Force, Khris Kellow, and Vassal Benford. Pearlman and Epic had gone out of their way to secure the cooperation of these musical masterminds for C-Note. And the guys couldn't have been more grateful. Secretly, they had been composing a wish list of the producers and writers with whom they wanted to collaborate. Imagine their surprise when most of their wishes were granted without them even having to ask.

Among the celebrated production roster was Guy Roche, who is credited with having cowritten Brandy's 1999 hit "Almost Doesn't Count." Also on the list was Vassal Benford, who'd produced eighties pop icon Sheena Easton, as well as Grammy winner Toni Braxton. The Full Force production team was also a major contributor to C-Note's album. Composed of members Shy, Baby Gerry, Curt-t, B-Fine, and Bowlegged Lou, that dream team is one of the most respected in the music industry. Having worked on hit albums for the likes of Lisa Lisa & the Cult Jam and Steven Dante, Full Force was bound to work some magic in the studio.

Another addition to C-Note's production list was an up-and-coming producer named Dakari, who would be working closely with C-Note every step of the way. And finally, Ginuwine. An R&B singer first and producer second, Ginuwine had recorded the double platinum album *Ginuwine . . . the Bachelor,* and in 1999, Ginuwine followed it up with *100% Ginuwine.*

Having this solo artist on board, along with the rest of the famed producers, was a tremendous coup for C-Note. The opportunity to work with these incredible music industry veterans was just what the guys needed to turn their debut album into a bona fide chart topper. "We got really lucky on this album," David explained during a *Soul Train* broadcast. "We got to work with a lot of great people."

From the outset, when they first joined their new production team in the studio, Raul, Brody, David, and Dru were concerned about what role they would have in the recording process. Everything was so new and exciting. The boys wanted to absorb all the lessons offered by the experts. Whether they were singing in the vocal booths or watching their producers man the boards, the group was always trying to pick up the tricks of the trade. For all they knew, this might be their one and only chance to study musical recording from the pros.

Unwilling just to sit by and watch everything happen, Raul, Brody, David, and Dru proved that they were true professionals by not letting anything escape their notice. Working round the clock to make their album the best it could be, the boys impressed all of their producers with their discipline and hard work. "Working with C-Note is a totally great experience as a producer," Dakari explained. "It was a collaborative thing. The guys are talented. C-Note is going to stand out. Their work ethic

is just so strong. The material is innovative. Their style
is . . . they just can't lose."

After a few weeks of working with the crack team of
producers, the guys became much more comfortable in
the studio. Pretty soon they had picked up what it takes
most people ages to learn. Offering input and making
adjustments, the group was instrumental in determining
the sound and style of their music. "We had such a good
opportunity to work with everybody," said Dru. "We can
all write and produce our own stuff as well, but we got
the opportunity to work with all these people and it
would have been silly not to take advantage of those
situations."

The more they learned, the more they wanted to contribute to their album. Unlike some artists who'd rather
hand over all the responsibility of production to the experts, the guys of C-Note took an active role in all the
proceedings. After all, it was their music, and like it or
not, they would have a say in the recording process.

When they weren't busy watching the goings-on in
the studio, the guys used their spare time to compose
their own songs. They were confident in their ability to
write a hit, and wanted the chance to prove themselves.
As the group confirmed to CNN, "We kind of concentrate more on the musicality of it. I think we write and
produce and we try to have more of a hands-on approach."

Although they were exhausted from the nonstop recording sessions, Raul, David, Brody, and Dru would
come together long after everyone else had gone to bed
to compose songs for their album. After filling up an
endless array of trash cans with their failed attempts, the
boys stumbled upon a tune called "Spanish Fly," which
they thought was a surefire hit.

The next day, they went into the studio and played
the song for their full-time producer, Dakari, who hadn't
even known they were planning to write anything for
the album. As soon as he heard the song, Dakari was all

smiles and applause. He praised the guys for their effort and they immediately set to work on producing what turned out to be one of the most popular songs on the entire album. "It's such a good thing that we had the opportunity to go in and actually do our song," said Dru.

With most of the tracks already cut, the guys still needed a few more songs to round out the album. That's when songwriter extraordinaire Diane Warren came on the scene. One of the most famous and prolific songwriters around, Diane Warren was responsible for writing hit songs for such artists as Aerosmith, Toni Braxton, Celine Dion, Joe Cocker, Roy Orbison, LeAnn Rimes, Monica, Whitney Houston, Barbra Streisand, Elton John, and many illustrious others. Warren's music has also been featured on over fifty motion picture soundtracks, and she has garnered many Grammy, Academy Award, and Golden Globe nominations along the way. During the 1998 Grammy Awards, three of the five songs nominated for Best of the Year were written by Warren.

Like most singers, David, Brody, Raul, and Dru had wanted to work with her for as long as they could remember. But Diane Warren wasn't in the habit of giving out her hits to just anybody. The group would have to meet with her beforehand, so she could decide which songs, if any, she would want to contribute. Before they met Warren, the group worried about making the right impression. The idea that she was even considering bestowing her lyrical gems on the group was mind-boggling; so much so that the guys thought that she would reject their appeal for new songs outright.

Instead of the dead serious and businesslike woman that they had imagined, Diane turned out to be a warm and down-to-earth person. Immediately smitten by the group's rousing performance, Diane told them, "yes!" They could record two of her songs, titled "Tell Me Where It Hurts" and "One Night with You."

For Brody, working with Warren was an experience

to remember. "My highlight was being able to meet Diane Warren and record some of her songs," he revealed to *Pop Star* magazine. "The first time I met her, she was like, 'These are the songs you are going to do. They are going to be hits.' Then when we came back and recorded them, she was sitting down with us, chewing the fat, eating Doritos with us, she put a bird on my shoulder. She is just a regular person. It seemed weird because I had her up on such a pedestal. That's it. She is the best songwriter in the world."

IT'S SHOW TIME

Once Diane Warren's songs had been recorded and fine-tuned, C-Note's inaugural album was finally ready for mass consumption. But even though they worked hard to complete their debut effort, Epic wasn't planning to release it until the summer of 1999. In the meantime, they had a lot more work to do. If they had any hopes of selling their album, they would have to build up a solid fan base by spreading word of their existence in advance. "It's not all, you know, OK let's put four guys together," the group told CNN. "Throw them out. They've got a record deal and that's it. I mean we've been busting our humps."

Since their first performance at the Tornado relief benefit, the guys had been too busy with recording the album to perform live. But now that their work in the studio was done, they were free to sing wherever and whenever they wanted.

Pearlman and manager Alan Siegal had not forgotten the great splash that C-Note had made at its debut concert. They wanted the guys to have as much exposure as possible and started booking gigs almost immediately. One of C-Note's first appearances was made at the Trans Continental Showcase at the House of Blues. Also scheduled to perform that night were Trans Con's very own Innosence and LFO.

The show opened with the group Innosence warming up the crowd with their smooth harmonies. But as soon as they had closed out their set, the packed crowd began chanting, "C-Note, C-Note, C-Note!" They'd had enough of the waiting, and demanded that the group make an appearance. While this was only their second performance, the quartet was already one of Trans Con's most popular acts.

David, Raul, Brody, and Dru were on fire that night. By the time they danced their last step and finished singing the crowd-pleasing "So Often," "My Heart Belongs to You," and "Wait Till I Get Home," the audience was in utter rapture. The spectators had grown so enamored with the foursome that the guys had no choice but to hang around after show, signing autographs and posing for photos with their fans.

With just two showcases under their collective belt, the guys felt like old pros. They couldn't wait to get back onstage, pestering manager Siegal to no end to let them perform more often. Unwilling to let his boys down, Siegal booked C-Note to sing at the closing ceremonies of Florida's Special Olympics. A very prestigious honor for any new act, the chance to sing in front of thousands of potential fans was not to be missed. Once the medals had been handed out, C-Note helped the crowd celebrate the achievements of the local Olympians. Spirits ran high all around as the C-Notes showed off their smooth vocals and some of their latest dance routines.

Although they had been the only performers at the Special Olympics, their next gig, singing at St. Petersburg's Fourth of July celebration, would require that they share the bill with another group—'N Sync.

Ever since their first performance with 'N Sync, Raul, David, Brody, and Dru had become good friends with the group's members. In turn, 'N Sync thought of the C-Note guys as brothers, and were always excited to cross paths with them. This occasion would be no exception. As soon as the groups arrived, they began catching up on the latest developments in each other's lives. They were so engrossed in the conversation that the guys of C-Note almost missed their cue. Luckily, as soon as the group was onstage, facing the thousands-strong throng that had gathered for the event, they regained their composure and delivered another earthshaking performance.

GETTING INTO THE ACT

While Independence Day went off without a hitch, there were times when the group experienced some very embarrassing moments. Of course, the very nature of live concerts is such that accidents are bound to happen. Brody is still trying to live down his worst mishap to date.

"We were doing a show in West Palm Beach and we parked a tour bus right next to this little stage," he revealed to America Online. "Right before the intro came on, we were supposed to run out of the bus and jump on stage. And so the intro kicks on and we were about to go out, and the first two guys get out of the bus just fine. When I tried to get over the step, I literally leaped forward and my suit tore and flew all over the place. I had to go on stage dancing and my suit was flying all over and I couldn't get the mike in the mike stand, and so I was holding it in my hand when the choreography was supposed to be with the mike stand. So I'm still seeing a therapist to get over that."

Dru has also had his brushes with public humiliation, the worst of which he recalled in *CosmoGirl!*: "I go down and shake it a lot. Once, I got offstage and realized my fly had been open the whole show. I was like, 'Okay . . . package everywhere!' "

Despite these awkward moments, there's no denying that getting onstage to be cheered on by thousands of people is a privilege reserved for only a select few. Try as they might, Raul, David, Dru, and Brody could not get used to the unconditional love afforded them by their avid fans. It was as if they still believed that they were nobodies instead of the extremely successful group that they had actually become. "We're new at this 'being out there' thing," David admitted to *Latin Girl* magazine. "We get a rush out of hearing everybody scream."

Pleasing the crowd had become an obsession for the guys. There were some days when they couldn't wait to get in front of an audience. The more comfortable they became singing live, the more they began to understand what being a performer was all about. Whereas before, they were mostly concerned about not making mistakes or fools of themselves, they were now preoccupied with making their fans happy.

When asked about what makes him the happiest, David replied, "Um . . . I guess meeting so many different people that enjoy what you do. Because you can enjoy what you are doing and not see the rewards, but to us, we can look out to the crowd and see the smiles on their faces because of what we're doing for them. That's the best, and I am on cloud nine."

HIGH HOPES

Watching their Trans Con family members rise to the top of the charts couldn't have been easy. While C-Note was still trying to get a leg up in the industry, the Backstreet Boys and 'N Sync were enjoying the kind of success C-Note could only dream about. "We look at Backstreet and 'N Sync, and we're in awe of what's going on with them," Raul explained to the *Los Angeles Times*. "I think about it all the time. I wonder, 'Can that be us?' "

But while the boys were excited about following in those groups' footsteps, they also took pride in the differences that set their group apart.

Having proven that they could compete with the industry's hottest acts, C-Note was getting restless. The guys couldn't wait until the release of their own album.

Also anxious about the upcoming debut were the men behind C-Note. Louis Pearlman and Alan Siegal were convinced that the group would stand out in the tough market. Besides their good looks and hot dance moves, C-Note had something other groups didn't—the ability to sing in both Spanish and English. "If I had one word to define C-Note that word would have to be diverse," commented Siegal. "Their bilingual, Hispanic heritage. They're a crossover into the Latin market, they're R&B style. The fact that all the guys can sing lead is something that was very appealing."

Today, Latin music has become the most *caliente* phenomenon to hit the music industry in years. With heavyweights such as Ricky Martin, Jennifer Lopez, and Enrique Iglesias crossing over to the English-speaking market, the time was ripe for C-Note's blend of music. Long before Ricky Martin had begun planning his U.S. invasion, the guys of C-Note were keeping it real with their Spanish verses and R&B harmonies. And even though singing in Spanish wasn't considered to be cool at the time, the guys of C-Note were determined to bring Latin music out of the closet. "Two or three years ago, it wasn't such a hot thing to do," David told *Latin Girl* magazine. "People would ask why we included Spanish in our songs, but that's who we are."

With their musical tastes ranging from Latin artists such as Celia Cruz, El Gran Combo, and Tito Puente to R&B crooners such as New Edition, Michael Jackson, and Boyz II Men, the guys had melded a unique sound that was bound to get noticed. As David informed *Teen* magazine, "Our music is not pop, it's not R&B, it's not Latin—it's the whole bunch mixed together."

Even Dru, who isn't of Hispanic descent, learned to love singing in Spanish as much as the rest of the group. "I enjoy singing in Spanish even more than I do in English," he explained. "It's more melodic."

While Dru may have fallen in love with the language, the Latin trio had other reasons for incorporating Spanish into their repertoire. Proud of their rich heritage, Brody, Raul, and David felt that it was their responsibility to raise awareness about their culture and to break down racial stereotypes that are still prevalent in America. They considered themselves the voice of a generation that might not otherwise have a chance to speak for itself.

"The Latin influence is what really sets us apart," Raul explained to *Latin Girl* magazine. "There are a lot of people like us, the second generation of people that came over from Spanish-speaking countries in Latin America and Caribbean. We felt a need for our generation's voice to be expressed through music."

The guys of C-Note were nothing if not serious about their music and the message that they hoped to spread throughout the world. But having learned a thing or two about the power of strategic marketing, David, Brody, Raul, and Dru wanted to develop something other than the well-scrubbed, boy-next-door image popularized by the likes of Hanson and 'N Sync. Being too similar to other pop acts was something that could hurt their careers, in the sense that consumers would not be able to differentiate them from the competition. To remedy the situation, C-Note adopted a sexier, more urban image than that favored by its forerunners.

Marketing, however, was only part of the rationale behind C-Note's overall presentation. The fact is that the C-Note four really were more sensually inclined than their boy band contemporaries. Even before they'd joined Trans Con, their music had the strong edge that is their trademark to this very day. Of course, the group didn't want to go overboard on the sexual overtones for fear of alienating some of their younger fans. So, in order to spread their message of love and tolerance to as many people as possible, C-Note decided to walk the fine line between seduction and good clean fun. "[Our] music has sexuality," Dru told *Knight Ridder* newspaper. "It's provocative. C-Note likes to get down. [Our music is] suggestive, but in a classy way. It's not dirty by any means."

With their signature sound, look, and marketing strategies all worked out, Raul, Brody, Dru, and David were confident that they were about to embark on a whole new era of their lives. The entertainment industry's heavily guarded doors seemed to have been thrown wide open, and they waited anxiously to take their place in music history. There was no turning back now, not that they would ever want to. "We're ready for the release date," Dru relayed to MTV. "We just want to get out there and show the world who C-Note is. And just have a good time with it, and have fun and to bring smiles to everybody's faces out there and put on a good show."

6

David

With his dark, brooding good looks and deep, baritone voice, it's no wonder that David gets a surplus of attention from the female fans. Whether he's moving his body to the beat or singing those oh-so soulful notes, in the eyes of his many fans, David can simply do no wrong.

But sexiness is only one of the many things that makes David one of the best people to be around. Ask any of his friends or family members an they'll tell you that there is infinitely more to him than meets the eye. A sensitive and creative young man, David strives to improve himself in every possible way. Whether it's working out his lean physique or developing his song-writing prowess, this is one guy who knows how to give it everything he's got.

FAMILY TIES

As a young boy growing up in Hoboken, New Jersey, David had the best of both worlds. Manhattan was only a stone's throw away from his family home, and David would spend his younger days daydreaming about his grand destiny in the Big Apple.

Of Cuban and Puerto Rican descent, David's parents Carlos and Ana Perez played a vital role in his upbringing, instilling in him a deep respect for his heritage. Although David was always a rambunctious kid, he was a quick study from the start, and committed many of his parents' lessons to memory. His mother, Ana, played a major role in shaping his creativity and drive to be successful. "She instilled in me my pride in everything I do, not to start something I couldn't finish, and never quit on your dreams or what you believe in."

Although David's clan was extremely close, times weren't always easy. The Perez family had its share of financial struggles, and David would sometimes have to make sacrifices in order to save money. And while some of his other friends were getting new clothes, video games, and sports equipment, David's parents could never afford the luxuries that other parents allowed their children. But instead of becoming resentful about his station in life, David always tried to look on the bright side. He saw how hard his father worked, and always admired his dedication to the family. "As I was growing up, I remember him doing whatever he had to do to take care of the family. No matter how bad it got, he always said and acted like everything was OK and, eventually, it was."

All in all, David's childhood was filled with wonderful memories of family gatherings and fun. Whatever they may have lacked in the financial department, the Perez family made up for in love and understanding. When asked to describe what made him the happiest, David replied, "My whole family back together in New Jersey, having Christmas dinner and partying into the night. When I was younger, my whole family was in New Jersey, not only my immediate family."

BACK TO SCHOOL

As David matured, he grew into one of the most attractive and athletic young guys in town. High school was a blast for the young man. For a while, it seemed like David had it all—good looks, tons of friends, and more girlfriends than he knew what to do with.

One of the most popular guys in school, he was the ultimate big man on campus. Playing point guard on his high school's basketball team couldn't have hurt him any, either. As the team's All State guard and MVP, David was never at a loss when it came to handling a basketball. Everywhere he went, students and faculty would congratulate him on having played a great game. Is it any wonder that today David is one of the most confident young men around?

Of course, no one is without their little insecurities. David's happens to be his "chicken legs." As he told *CosmoGirl!*, "I played basketball, but the shorts were so short—and my legs have never been built. Everyone said I looked like a toothpick."

Despite this one minor drawback, David loved to play on the court and practice his jump shot. Still, something continued to interest him even more. When he was just a little boy, David found out he had a gift for dancing. He practiced day and night on perfecting his steps, but never knew what to do with his skills. Of course, his coordination and dancing skills paid off big time on the court. As graceful as a panther, he could whisk past even the toughest opponent and leave him in a cloud of dust.

Yet dancing continued to be his secret passion. During his senior year in high school, David was offered a full athletic scholarship. According to everyone he talked to, this was his ticket to greener pastures. His family could not afford to send him to college, and this was David's only chance to snag a college degree. While his entire family laid on the pressure big time, David had plans of his own.

When forced to choose between being a performer and a basketball player, David chose the former. Much to his family's chagrin, he announced that he would be moving to Orlando to pursue a life in show business.

Disappointed as they were, his parents supported his decision and prayed for the best.

Needless to say, David has never regretted making that decision.

GOING FOR IT

Once he landed in Orlando, David was quick to adapt to his new environment. Within a month, he'd made new friends, found a new apartment, and even scored a job.

But he had bigger plans still. No sooner was he settled than he began choreographing dance combinations and entering local competitions. Winning one prize after another, David soon became just as popular on the dance competition circuit as he had been on the high school scene. He was never without a dance partner, and loved to go out on the town.

Unfortunately, no matter how successful he was at dancing, talent scouts were not knocking down his door. Since most of the local entertainment gigs required vocal skills, David decided that he would have to learn how to sing. While he'd never shown any interest in singing before, necessity proved the mother of invention once again, giving rise to David's signature deep bass voice. "It was a dream of mine to be in the entertainment industry," he explained to *Pop Star!* "I always thought that it would be dancing or acting. But *singing*, I always thought was the furthest one."

It was lucky for David that he'd had the foresight to develop his voice, because when Raul and Brody invited him to join the group, he was ready and able to make his own valuable contribution to the group's sound. David has become such a tremendous singer that people are actually amazed to learn that he hasn't been doing it all of his life.

LADIES' MAN

David is the type of guy who seems to have lived his entire life without ever once having had so much as a bad hair day. In fact, it's quite probable that this is the only time you'll ever see the words "awkward" and "David Perez" appear in the same sentence. Maybe it's the way he dances, maybe it's the way he smolders on the stage—whatever it is, one thing is for certain: David's got that certain *je ne sais quoi*.

And even though he's had quite a number of girl-friends along the way, David is not a player. Behind his rugged demeanor beats the heart of a highly sensitive and romantic young man. "I'm romantic," he told *CosmoGirl!* "I just don't think anyone sees that side of me—except the girl I want to romance."

Indeed, David is pretty much the ideal boyfriend for any girl. He is generous, kind, and judging by his idea of the perfect rendezvous, will always go the extra mile for the girl of his dreams. "Candlelight dinner, then a basketball game, following that with some dancing," he explained. "After that, chill in a Jacuzzi with some champagne overlooking the ocean on a cool summer night." Now that's romantic.

Unfortunately, life on the road doesn't leave David with much time for romance. Although he deeply craves the affection of a long-term and stable relationship, his jam-packed travel itinerary has put his love life in the penalty box. Eventually, however, he hopes to settle down with his ideal woman in a picture-perfect setting. Describing his fantasy: "When I decide to settle down, finding my soul mate, and spending the rest of my life traveling and enjoying life to the fullest. And, always living for the moment."

FAST FACTS

Full Name: Eren David Perez

Nicknames: Dave, D'Lo, D.L.O.

Age: 26

Height: 6' 0"

Weight: 163 lbs.

Shoe Size: 12

Birthday: September 21

Astrological Sign: Virgo

Pet: Rottweiler: D'Keepa (short for David's Keeper)

Favorite Album: LL Cool J, L L Cool J

Favorite Concerts: BBD, Keith Sweat

Favorite Toothpaste: Crest

Favorite Song: "Victory," Puff Daddy and Notorious B.I.G.

Favorite Food: Breaded steak, rice, and red beans

Favorite Cartoon: Thundercats

Favorite Animal: Dog

Favorite Sport: Basketball

Favorite Sports Team: Orlando Magic

Favorite Drink: Welch's Grape Juice

Favorite Game: 007 for N64

Favorite Colors: Black and Silver

Favorite Car: Lexus Land Cruiser

Favorite Cologne: Jean Paul Gaultier

Favorite Movie: Scarface

7

Dru

As C-Note's resident blond and the only member who is not of Hispanic descent, it would appear that Dru might have had some trouble fitting in with the boys. But nothing could have been further from the truth. Dru is the kind of guy that girls love and guys admire. Always willing to laugh at himself and play the goofball, he has a way of putting people at ease wherever he goes. "I'm the comedian type," he told *CosmoGirl!*, "so I'm always looking to make people laugh."

Still, to label him the class clown and leave it at that would be unfair. A complex and serious young man, Dru's waters run very deep—so deep that his friends would never dare hurt his feelings, for fear of offending him. All things considered, Dru's addition to the group is one of the best things that could have happened to Raul, Brody, and Dave. Dru has become such a vital part of the act that they are often at their wits' end wondering where they'd be without him.

RAISING DRU

Born Andrew Michael Rogers in the quiet suburb of Red Bank, New Jersey, Dru lived the kind of idyllic lifestyle most kids can only see on TV. With a brother and sister, young Dru was never at a loss for amusement. The three kids would often play together after school, and are still the best of friends to this very day.

The close relationship between the children may have something to do with the fact that their parents were the kindest and most giving of people. Always willing to give their son whatever his heart desired, Raymond and Valerie Rogers were completely devoted to raising Dru in the best way possible. Even today, Dru brags about the close bond he shares with his family. He knows full well that if it wasn't for their unconditional support and affection he may have never made it as far as he has. Dru wants to thank "my father Ray and my mother Valerie for the terrific upbringing and family I am so fortunate to be a part of." He continued, "You all are my life and my heroes."

The Rogers wanted Dru to make something out of himself, so when he asked to play an instrument at an early age, they agreed. After picking out a guitar, Dru would practice until the morning hours, driving his poor parents crazy in the process. "Actually, I've been a musician my whole life," Dru noted. "I started playing guitar when I was like five. I played in school bands and the drums here and there."

Even though they were inconvenienced by his playing, Dru's mom and dad would never have thought to take away the instrument that made him happy. Because of their consistent encouragement, he learned all about music—not just the guitar, but drums as well. "My interest in music began right in Middletown," Dru said, "when I started playing the drums."

But Dru's musical adventures didn't begin and end in New Jersey. He carried on with his instruments even after the Rogers family moved to Orlando when Dru was still in fourth grade.

A STAR IS BORN

It was in high school that Dru finally hit upon his destiny. He had always loved music, but had never tried to sing, except alone in the shower. Like David, Dru spent most of his time in the pursuit of athletic excellence. "I never took anything seriously except athletics: football, track and basketball."

One day, however, all that would change. While Dru was hanging out with some buddies, one of his friends, Gary, started goofing off and singing. At first, the guys were somewhat taken aback, but as curious onlookers flocked to the source of the music, the guys began to bask in the attention. Everyone was amazed with Gary's voice, and clapped loudly when his impromptu show was over.

Seeing the kind of impression his friend had made on the small audience, Dru was in awe of his talent. Wow! Would he ever love to be able to sing like that. In congratulating his friend for a job well done, Dru realized how much he wanted to learn to sing—not so much for the attention, but in order to make people as happy as Gary did that day. The idea had never occurred to him before, but once it did, he immediately asked his buddy to teach him a thing or two.

Today, whenever he is asked about the one person who's made the biggest impact on his life, Dru always thinks back to that one fateful day. "My high school friend Gary Rowe who I heard sing once and was mesmerized," he explained. "If it hadn't been for him, I would never had started singing. Thanks, brother."

Practicing day and night, Dru found that singing was much harder than it looked. Eventually, he got up enough courage to sing at a show. But even though his first time out wasn't all it was cracked up to be (he claims to have bombed), Dru never wanted to give up singing. In fact, his confidence in his own abilities soon escalated to the point where he actually had the nerve to sing the national anthem at one of his high school football games. According to his grandmother Gertrude Rogers, the singing took everyone by surprise. "I couldn't imagine he did that," she said. "But he was involved in so many things. He's a trip, let me tell you."

Upon graduation, Dru became heavily involved in choirs and singing with various local groups. His brother, Scott, was also hit by the show-biz bug, and the two brothers joined one group after another in hopes of striking it big.

Eventually, Dru met up with Raul and the two began singing in the same group. Unfortunately for Raul, when Dru's brother called to ask Dru to join a group in Boston, he rushed to his side.

When that group broke up, he returned to Orlando and met up with the rest of the guys from C-Note, and the rest, as they say, is history. Recounting his path to stardom, Dru recalled, "I started singing with choral groups. I started getting interested in the musicality as far as arranging harmonies—different kinds of stuff like that— and then I started singing in various groups and met these guys along the way."

IT'S ALL ABOUT THE MUSIC

While some singers go into the business for money, girls, or fame, Dru didn't care about anything other than making great music. Just think about all the instruments he learned to play before he was even in high school: drums, guitar, bass, trumpet. Dru knew everything there was to know about music, and once he perfected his vocals, he realized that there was no telling how far his talent could take him.

While Latin music had never figured into either his repertoire or his CD collection, Dru could point to any number of musicians who influenced his current musical style. He listened to the classic soul favored by his parents, such as Stevie Wonder; George Benson; Earth, Wind and Fire; and Norman Brown. But once he heard the guys of C-Note sing their smooth harmonies, he was instantly carried away by the sound. "I grew up listening to a lot of funk, jazz, and R&B," he told *Teen* magazine. "As for the Latin thing, I'm learning as I go along."

Although he was the last to join the group, Dru found that he had a lot in common with Brody, Raul, and David. He had been in enough musical groups to know that this was the one with which he would be the most compatible. Because the group made sure that the music should always come first, before image or showmanship, Dru knew that he had finally found the group to which he could commit himself wholeheartedly.

Today, Dru is like a kid in a candy store. Being able to produce and write his own music has been extremely rewarding for him. He has also been able to meet many of his idols face-to-face. Unfortunately, he has yet to meet the one artist that he most admires. But with things going as well as they are, there's no telling what will happen in the future. When asked about the one person he would like to meet, Dru replied without hesitation: "Stevie Wonder. I'd just like to talk to him about life and where he gets his musical ideas and influences."

FAST FACTS

Full Name: Andrew Michael Rogers

Nickname: Dru

Height: 6' 0"

Weight: 165 lbs.

Shoe Size: 10

Birthplace: Red Bank, New Jersey

Birthday: July 19

Astrological Sign: Cancer

Pets: Dogs: Morgan and Nala

Hometown: Red Bank, New Jersey

Favorite Artist: Stevie Wonder

First Concerts: M.C. Hammer, Kiss

Favorite Toothpaste: Mentadent

Favorite Song: "Send Your Love," Stevie Wonder

Favorite Food: Canoli

Favorite Cartoon: Bugs Bunny

Favorite Animal: Koala Bear

Favorite Sports: Football, Track, Soccer

Favorite Sports Team: Green Bay Packers

Favorite Drink: Pepsi

Favorite Video Game: Manx GT

Favorite Color: Blue

Favorite Car: Plymouth Prowler

Favorite Cologne: CK One

Favorite Movie: The American President

8

Raul

By now, you probably know everything there is to know about C-Note. But what about the man who is responsible for bringing all of the group's members together? With his tenacious drive and dedication to the group, Raul Molina has become the undisputed leader of the pack of four.

After all, it was his decision to bring David onboard after seeing him dance at his sister's sweet sixteen party. Besides that, Raul could be credited with finding Dru since both had been in a group together before. From day one, Raul has been the glue that has kept C-Note from unhinging ("Just call me Elmer's," he jokes). His keen business sense, maturity, and ceaseless drive to sing are what make Raul one of the most interesting guys in the group.

BORN TO SING

While Raul's group mates didn't discover the joys of belting out a tune until they hit their teens, Raul was singing long before his wonder years. Born in Santo Domingo, Dominican Republic, Raul was brought to the United States by his parents when he was just a little boy. Once his parents had immigrated, they realized that making their way in America would not be as easy as they'd originally thought. During Raul's childhood, times were hard for the Molina family, and they tried to get by the best way they could.

Raul still remembers those days of hardship when the family had to scrimp and save in order to eat. It is this vivid memory that follows him to this very day, motivating him to succeed. "My parents are the most influential people in my life," he revealed. "I believe that they have lived through a lot, and can help me out with what they have learned. To see how hard they worked to make sure that we had what we needed was truly heroic."

Not only did his parents endow the young boy with the ambition to carve out a better future, they taught him the importance of spirituality. It was actually in church, when Raul was only four years old, that he first felt the power of music to heal and uplift. "There's nothing like singing in church, like singing for God, but it all comes from the same place," Raul told *Latin Girl* magazine. "It's still coming from inside of us, still something we believe in."

Seeing that their son had a gift for music, Raul's parents wasted no time in giving him lessons and encouraging him to perform. Soon, everyone in the Molina circle knew of Raul's gift. Whenever the chance presented itself, there he'd be, whooping it up for his parents and their friends.

During family gatherings, the young boy would often entertain the party by imitating his favorite performer, John Travolta. "Whenever *Grease* would come on TV or *Saturday Night Fever*, I would perform those moves—the John Travolta parts—for friends and my family," he explained. "It would be like a thing. If it was going to come on at eight, they would all get ready and I would go up front and do a whole thing."

While performing Travolta's notorious steps one night, Raul had a terrible accident that required him to get stitches on his head. In an attempt to copy his idol, Raul had executed a back flip off his mother's bed and hit his head on the windowsill. After being rushed to the hospital, the young boy promised to get a new act going.

THE PATH TO GLORY

No amount of stitches, however, could stop Raul from doing the one thing he loved most. From the ages of nine to sixteen, he would practice his singing and then compete in local talent shows. The judges were always struck by his amazing vocal range, and encouraged him to continue singing. For Raul, the attention was the biggest draw. "I was a chubby kid," he explained to *CosmoGirl!* "Singing was my way to get people to notice me."

And notice him they did. In high school, Raul was considered to be one of the most well-rounded young men around. Not only did he sing and get good grades, he was also one of the best basketball players on his team.

But it was his singing that earned him a prestigious music scholarship to college. When he was offered the scholarship, Raul and his family celebrated the momentous occasion. Since the scholarship would enable Raul to pursue his passion while getting a college education at the same time, his parents were especially relieved.

University living, however, failed to expand Raul's career horizons. He was dead set on singing his life away. While there were those naysayers who tried to push Raul into a "legitimate" profession, he was convinced that his voice would see him through.

It was in college that Raul first ran into Brody. The two became good friends and sang together in a variety of groups. While Raul knew that he would become successful one day, Brody had his doubts and left the group to concentrate on school. But even though Raul was also breaking his back trying to keep up his grades and work odd jobs on the side, he refused to accept defeat.

HERE AND NOW

Today, Raul is overwhelmed by everything that has happened to him. Whenever a fan comes up to ask for his autograph or when he's recognized in the street, Raul thinks back to a time when he was just a little boy trying to disco dance in his parents' living room. His days as a struggling artist, when he had to hold down part-time jobs to make ends meet, are also gone but not forgotten. If those meager beginnings ever did slip his mind, the girls whom he used to work with as a girls' basketball coach would surely remind him. "Now the girls call me and say, 'So-and-so doesn't believe that I know you,' " Raul told *CosmoGirl!* "I have to tell their friends, 'Yeah, it's me.' "

Part of what makes Raul such a charismatic young man is the support and loyalty he has for the group he helped form. And don't think that Brody, David, and Dru don't thank their lucky stars that Raul had enough courage to stick with music when they had all but given up.

No doubt it is this drive and dedication to music that is responsible for much of C-Note's success. Still, Raul doesn't mind admitting that all the ambition in the world would not have been enough had it not been for his loyal fans. He is so grateful to have supporters that he is always coming up with ways to do something nice for them. Be it staging a show or offering to pose for pictures, Raul is never too tired to go the extra mile for his fans. And judging by all his fan mail, his efforts have not gone unnoticed.

FAST FACTS

Full Name: Raul Emilio Molina

Nicknames: Rolo, RaRa

Height: 5' 11"

Weight: 185 lbs.

Shoe Size: 10

Birthplace: Dominican Republic

Birthday: April 30

Astrological Sign: Taurus

First Album: Grease—Motion Picture Soundtrack

First Concert: Boyz II Men

Favorite Toothpaste: Crest

Favorite Food: Rice, red beans, and bistec

Favorite Cartoon: Pinky & The Brain

Favorite Animal: Horse

Favorite Sport: Basketball

Favorite Sports Teams: Orlando Magic, San Francisco 49ers

Favorite Drink: Coke

Favorite Video Game: Metal Gear Solid

Favorite Color: Blue

Favorite Car: Dodge Viper

Favorite Cologne: Curve by Liz Claiborne

Favorite Movie: The Godfather trilogy

Favorite City: Orlando

9
Brody

To his true-blue fans, multitalented Brody needs no introduction, but those who don't follow his every move with the vigilance of a federal agent may need to get the info on this adorable singer.

Brody is probably the shyest and most laid-back member of the group. Even when the pressure is on, he always tries to stay calm and exercise self-control. The only sweat he ever breaks is when he's dancing onstage.

Brody is also a real lady-killer when he wants to be. For those people who have yet to receive the full Brody treatment, you should know that he is one of the biggest flirts in the group. Always willing to give a wink or a dazzling smile to his many fans, Brody has a way of making a girl's heart go pitter-patter. So if you want to know more about what makes this Latin heartthrob tick, read on to discover all of the juicy details of his life.

UPS AND DOWNS

Few people know this, but Brody was not always this happy-go-lucky. Born José Antonio Martinez III in San Juan, Puerto Rico, the young boy had the perfect life, until he experienced a serious tragedy that haunts him to this very day. When Brody was only five years old, his mother passed away. Needless to say, he and the rest of his family, including all of his brothers and sisters, had a hard time dealing with the loss. Brody was especially close to her, and spent most of his time mourning his mother's memory. "She died when I was five and I have always dreamt about knowing her better," he explained. "I wish I would have had more time with her."

Brody and his family tried to recover as best as they could. It was up to his father to bring up the kids, and try to fill the shoes of two parents. Although being a single parent couldn't have been easy, he managed to provide the emotional and financial stability that helped the children weather the storm.

Growing up by his father's side, young Brody learned to admire his dad's steadfastness and reliability. In fact, he so admires his father that he tries to emulate him whenever possible. "My father is the most influential person in my life," he said. "He's always set me on the right path. And, he's always—no matter how nasty I've been—been in my corner."

Since his childhood was fraught with so much difficulty, Brody took to singing around the house to lift his spirits. Even though he thought he had a nice voice, he never seriously considered the prospect of making a living as a singer. To Brody, singing was a way of passing the time. To his sneaky siblings, however, Brody's vocals were the source of much amusement. "My earliest memory is singing in my shower," he told *Pop Star* magazine. "My little sisters and brothers would bring their friends up to the door to listen to me. But I was more into baseball than I was into anything else."

Brody was indeed a fanatic when it came to America's favorite pastime. Playing in Little League was just about the most rewarding experience of his young life, and he dreamed of one day entering the majors. Today, his hero continues to be one of the most respected baseball legends in the world. "Roberto Clemente would have to be my hero because he died trying to help others," responded Brody. "He was a great baseball player, a great talent, but most of all, he was a great human being."

ON HIS OWN

During his senior year in high school, Brody was shipped off to live with his aunt in Michigan because his father wanted him to have the best education possible. And while the academic program was top-notch, Brody had a hard time fitting into his new school. Being the new kid is never easy, but it was especially difficult on Brody, whose shy nature had never won him any schoolyard popularity contests.

In order to make new friends, he decided to join an extracurricular activity. That's when he saw flyers for the school choir. He remembered how much he had liked singing as a little boy, and decided to give the choir a shot.

Little did he know that he had all but sealed his fate with that one decision. Besides making plenty of new friends, Brody, with the help of his instructors, discovered that he had an incredible voice. With a little work, he soon became one of the choir's brightest stars. For the first time in his life, Brody felt like he was a part of something special, something that made him truly happy.

Prior to senior year, the idea of being a vocalist had never even presented itself. Choir helped him find his calling, and he set his sights on a singing career. But the young man would have to make up for lost time if he wanted to pursue singing in college. It's a lucky thing he joined the choir when he did, because he just made the cutoff point to submit his application for a musical scholarship.

When he was finally accepted into the college where he would later meet Raul, Brody was more surprised than anyone. He was amazed with himself for having the courage to pursue and realize his newfound dream.

GIRLS, GIRLS, GIRLS

As a young boy, Brody wasn't very comfortable around girls. While most guys were playing the field, he was just trying to get up the nerve to talk to girls. Watching him in action now, it's clear that the tables have turned. As a member of one of the most alluring pop groups in the world, Brody has no trouble meeting girls. In fact, he is surrounded by more girls than he can handle. He is so thrilled with his new crushworthy status that he rarely misses an opportunity to flirt with his many female fans.

But what qualities does Brody look for in a girl? Well, you'd be surprised to find out that he has a very specific type in mind, unlike the rest of the group, who aren't as discriminating. "I like brunettes with brown eyes and copper-toned skin," he confided in *Latin Girl*. "Petite girls about 5" 4' or 5" 5'. I'm a one-girl guy. In fact, I want a girlfriend, but this isn't the right time. . . . You need time together for your relationship to grow."

While Brody obviously thinks good looks are important, he is quick to admit that superficial charms are only part of the love equation. When it comes to long-term relationships, he is as serious-minded as they come. Keeping love alive requires a lot more than a pretty face, and Brody understands this better than anybody. "Without trust, there's nothing," he confirmed. "I like having total trust with my partner. I like knowing that we can tell each other anything and not play the 'secret game.' "

While he may enjoy the exhilaration of having thousands of girls hanging on his every lyric, Brody's dream is to one day find the woman who will mean everything to him. Unfortunately, he knows that that day won't come around anytime in the immediate future.

His schedule and professional demands require that

he fly from one city to the next at a moment's notice. And since few girls would ever put up with such long absences, even for Brody, he has no choice but to wait and be patient. "Being on the road, doing what we do, it's not like we don't want girlfriends," he told America Online. "We just can't find ones to keep us but maybe a month or two. A girl can't handle it, they're like, 'You're never home!' "

FAST FACTS

Full Name: José Antonio Martinez III

Nicknames: Brody, Brodifius

Height: 5' 8"

Weight: 163 lbs.

Shoe Size: 9

Birthplace: San Juan, Puerto Rico

Birthday: February 27

Astrological Sign: Pisces

Pet: Dog: Lucky

First Album: Parents Just Don't Understand, Will Smith

First Concert: Aerosmith

Favorite Toothpaste: Crest

Favorite Song: "Anytime," Brian McKnight

Favorite Food: Italian

Favorite Cartoon: X-Men

Favorite Animal: Cheetah

Favorite Sport: Baseball

Favorite Sports Team: Detroit Lions

Favorite Drink: Sprite

Favorite Video Game: EA's Baseball 99

Favorite Color: Green

Favorite Car: Navigator

Favorite Cologne: Wings

Favorite Movie: The Godfather trilogy

Favorite City: London

10

Breaking Out

C-Note had it all. A top-notch management team, a supportive network of friends and family, and the prospects for a long and lucrative career in pop music. With so many things working in their favor, you'd think Raul, Brody, Dru, and David would begin to get complacent or find time to relax before the big debut. But the boys weren't about to leave anything to chance.

The year 1999 would see the group busier than ever, from being interviewed on live radio to performing in media showcases to signing records for their fans. No matter how much success came C-Note's way, the guys knew that the harder they worked, the better their odds for breaking into pop music big time.

SOUND OF SUCCESS

Good publicity is hard to come by, especially when a group has even yet to release a single. But C-Note was once again the exception to most rules. In January 1999, the group received a significant boost from the friendly folks at MTV when the network aired C-Note on the acclaimed program, *Ultra Sound*. As the newest addition to the boy band genre, C-Note received the full press treatment. They were interviewed on camera, and even gave MTV a tour through the Trans Con facility.

The guys loved seeing themselves on national television, especially when they knew millions of viewers would watch them going through the motions of their daily lives. Little did they know, but the appearances would spark a craze for everything C-Note. After seeing the group that was waiting in the wings of the music industry, viewers began calling MTV to find out how they could get the group's music and where to send fan mail.

Unfortunately, the guys of C-Note had yet to release their debut album, and their new fans had to content themselves with checking out the group's official website. Before the series aired, C-Note's website was averaging around seven hundred hits per day. But that all changed after the program, when the site began receiving over four thousand hits each day.

The ever-expanding fan base even began to mobilize their HTML skills in order to build new C-Note shrines. In the months that followed their first nationally televised interview, the group was honored with a handful of personal web pages devoted to chronicling their every step.

When Epic Records saw how much devotion the group elicited through just one television appearance, they began beefing up the group's promotional campaign. The extensive radio tour, television appearances, mall stops, and record store signings showed that the people at Epic were serious about putting the group front and center.

But money can only buy so much. And Epic knew that all the marketing in the world couldn't replace radio station support. For new artists, getting airplay is one of the toughest challenges of their careers. DJs are very particular about the kind of music they play, and are usually not as accepting of new artists.

For their lead single, C-Note selected "Wait Till I Get Home" for its radio-friendly vibe. Epic executives sent the single to hundreds of radio stations, and to everyone's great relief the single was soon being played on over fifty radio stations nationwide.

One of the most memorable events in the career of any musical group is hearing their song on the radio for the first time. When the guys first caught their song blasting from their car radio, they were blown away. "The first time we were together it was a pretty beautiful scene," Raul revealed during an America Online chat. "We were all just going crazy. We were crying. That's what the 'C' stands for . . . Crybabies!"

Next on C-Note's busy agenda was to make its first video for "Wait Till I Get Home." Raul, Brody, David, and Dru were really psyched about taping their first video. They had been watching MTV for as long as they could remember, and, in their minds, having a video to call their very own was synonymous with pop stardom.

Although they were novices in the video-making department, Brody, Raul, David, and Dru had very firm ideas about what they did and did not want. When the director had outlined the concept for the visual extravaganza, the guys were pleased with his ideas. Of course they, along with their record company, also got to put in their two cents.

Once all of the suggestions had been incorporated, the guys were ready to unveil their first video to the world. "We just filmed the video about three weeks ago," explained Raul. "It just got done with editing. We had to go back and forth with what we liked, what the record label liked and what the director liked and you should be seeing it very shortly."

The video's premise was to have Raul, Brody, Dru, and David act like four friends having the time of their life while cruising the streets in their deluxe convertible. Along the way, the four amigos catch sight of some girls, and immediately follow them to a nearby coffee shop. When they get there, the girls are already inside sipping their beverages. That's when the guys decide to lure them out of the shop by dancing and serenading them. Needles to say, the girls can't resist this fabulous foursome, and go out to the alley where they all begin to dance with one another. But these aren't your average, run-of-the-mill dance steps. Extremely suggestive and sexy, all of the guys prove that they can get down with the best of them. From the alley, the camera takes the boys to a parking lot, where they once again meet with their damsels. Then, the whole group breaks into what is one of the coolest dance numbers we've ever seen. A wild and colorful video, "Wait Till I Get Home" was one of the most popular selections on The Box and even made it to Wannabe status on MTV.

THE MOMENT OF TRUTH

On Tuesday, May 25, 1999, *A Different Kind of Love* was finally released to the stores. With so much riding on their first album, the guys began to feel the pressure that went hand in hand with being the new kids on the proverbial block. Would their album sell, or disappear without so much as a nod from *Billboard*? Although the debut wasn't what they'd hoped it would be (*A Different Kind of Love* failed to enter into *Billboard* Top One Hundred), the guys were optimistic about improving their chart position, especially when they read some of the stellar CD reviews written by the toughest critics in the music business.

For many acts, critical acclaim is often just as important as selling records. For the C-Note guys, a good review meant that their music had not gone unappreciated—they were finally gaining acceptance in the music industry. While most of America had yet to familiarize themselves with C-Note, the reviews were a clear sign that the guys were earning respect as artists. They were also bound to draw more fans through the positive feedback. Either way, a good write-up seemed like the answer to their prayers.

A music reviewer for the industry's leading entertainment magazine, *Entertainment Weekly*, couldn't help but acknowledge their favorite singles from *A Different Kind of Love*, writing, "They do have one irresistible single, 'Wait Till I Get Home,' cowritten by Full Force. You'll also find a few more aggressive ditties than on most such efforts."

But even better praise was on its way from a critic at E! Online, whose assessment ran as follows: "This Orlando foursome is smooth and toothsome . . . and the tunes written by Full Force, including 'My Heart Belongs to You,' are as slickly romantic as Top 40 gets."

A reporter from *The Atlanta Constitution* was especially impressed with the group's Latin vibe, writing, "With the recent success of Ricky Martin and other Latin-tinged popsters, the timing couldn't be better. Most of the music here is standard-issue R&B lite, but the slight tropical flavor is more than welcome. 'Spanish Fly' is miles ahead of the other tracks in almost every way, and, not coincidentally, it has a very pronounced Latin groove."

HARD DAY'S NIGHT

With plenty of good reviews to call their own, the guys were ready to launch the stateside radio and press tour that would help them secure an even wider fan base. Their promotional tour included everything from being interviewed by DJs to posing for magazine layouts to signing albums at record stores.

Always partial to traveling, C-Note was enthusiastic about launching the countrywide trek. Little did the guys know that a promotional tour would require them to work harder than ever. "The weird thing about it is, beginning with our signing with Trans Con, then a year later with Epic, was that everything seemed to happen in gradual stages," Raul informed Gavin.com. "We kind of expected it, but nothing can prepare you to jump into promotion for a record. We get up at four A.M., hit two or three radio stations, with no real time to eat or sleep, then get to bed around one A.M. and start all over. No matter how many times people tell you about it, you really can't be prepared for it. Once the record came out, the pace really started to pick up."

Raul, Brody, David, and Dru never expected that a performer's life could be so hectic. They had always dreamed of getting swept up in a whirlwind lifestyle, but now that it was really happening, they were not prepared to deal with some of the disadvantages that went along with life in the fast lane.

Homesickness for their family and friends back home proved to be the main gripe. Because they were on the road twenty-four hours a day seven days a week, the guys, who are extremely tight with their families and close friends, missed being able to visit whenever the mood struck. "With me it would have to be the traveling and being away from home," Raul told America Online. "It's something that we knew would happen, but it's something that we weren't really ready for. Even when you're at home you don't have time to see your friends. You make time for your family, of course, but there's so little time that you don't get to see your friends and a little bit of sleep."

Of course, there were also plenty of benefits to being on a promotional tour. Wherever they went, the guys felt like pop music royalty. Everyone they met, from radio executives to magazine editors, rolled out the red carpet for their arrival. The group was also getting the chance to get up close and personal with many of their fans, who would sometimes travel long distances just to catch a glimpse of the guys along the way. One time, these very fans made the unthinkable happen. "We were staying in the same hotel as 'N Sync," Brody recalled in *CosmoGirl!*, "and there were girls outside saying, 'We want to see C-Note!'"

All in all, the publicity experience was like launching an extensive political campaign, except that in this case the guys were trying to win over music buyers instead of voters. "The hours are demanding, you have no control over your time and there is no time to eat—and eating is very important to us! But it's the best job in the world," Raul asserted to *Teen* magazine. "We used to sit in my room and talk about it till three in the morning, and now we're doing it."

NOT JUST ANOTHER PRETTY FACE

Dozens of radio, magazine, and newspaper interviews later, the guys had become old hands at handling the question-and-answer sessions that so many celebs have to go through. But no matter how many times they'd undergone the routine, there was one question that never failed to unnerve them. Whether or not C-Note considered itself to be a "boy band" was the one query that found its way into nearly every conversation. And, truth be told, Raul, Brody, David, and Dru were tired of this line of inquiry. "People are going to categorize us wherever they want to put us," explained Raul. "For now, wherever they want to put us, that is fine for now. But when they get to see the show and hear the music they'll realize there's a separate C-Note category."

Although they didn't mind being compared to the Backstreet Boys and 'N Sync when it came to the Louis Pearlman connection, they defended themselves when reporters tried to compare their musical style with that of other groups. Sure, they sing, dance, and share the same musical family but, according to C-Note, that's where the similarities end.

"The only way that you can compare us to other similar bands is that we are four guys that sing and dance. That's it," David conveyed to *Latin Girl* magazine.

"This is an organic group. We don't want to be seen as somebody's newest creation, 'cause that's not what we're about. This is something that we feel, something that we love. We want everyone to feel that the moment they pop in the CD."

No one was more displeased by these constant comparisons than the people at Epic, who knew firsthand that the group had just as much substance as they had style. "First and foremost," Ceci Kurzman, Epic's VP of marketing, told *Billboard* magazine, "we don't see them as a boy group, but as a very talented vocal group. It just so happens that they're also very good-looking."

Epic, of course, was not in the habit of giving out record contracts to every studly group of guys that walked in the door. Raul, Brody, David, and Dru knew that it was not their appearance but their talent that had won them the deal. So while they resented the media's implication that they were a manufactured act, the guys were secure enough in their own abilities to remain calm. "If we were ugly, then maybe our music would be taken seriously," Raul told the *Knight Ridder* newspaper. "Once people get past the fact that we're good-looking, they're going to be left with our talent. They'll judge it based on that."

ALL FOR THE FANS

Try to find another group who's as committed to making their fans happy as C-Note is, and you may find yourself searching until the end of time. Whether it's because they're new to the business or just love to hear their admirers scream, the group is not likely to take their hard-won constituency for granted anytime soon.

Raul, David, Brody, and Dru never miss an opportunity to give back to the fans who have already given them so much. While other groups try to shirk the responsibilities of signing autographs and taking pictures, the guys in C-Note grab every chance to show their fans

how much they mean to them. And if that means stand-
ing for hours on their sore feet to smile at the camera,
then that is exactly what they are prepared to do.

While all of their fans share the common link of loyalty, C-Note's fans are unlike any other group's in that
they come from a variety of different age and ethnic
groups. C-Note prides itself on making the kind of music
that appeals to all types of people from all types of backgrounds. As David explained, "So many different kinds
of people groove with us, which is great because we
want our music to cross the barriers of age, color, race,
whatever."

After performing at countless concerts and signing a
mountain of autographs, the guys were surprised to find
that older women were coming out to see them in
droves. Even though many of them came with their
daughters, they were instantly smitten with the guys.
"The group doesn't really have a core audience," Ceci
Kurzman explained to *Billboard*. "They attract teens,
people in their 20s, as well as women in their 30s and
40s. It's like the mothers are insisting on attending the
shows with their daughters."

The guys were shocked by this revelation. Not that
they doubted their ability to draw women of all ages,
but they were taken aback by the sheer zeal of their older
female fans. "After each show, we sign autographs, and
there'll be mothers waiting on line with their daughters,"
noted Raul. "And it's always the mothers who do the
most flirting. It's like the mothers are living vicariously
through their daughters, reliving their youth. We have a
lot of fun with it."

Guys are also not exempt from jumping on the C-
Note bandwagon. Raul, David, Brody, and Dru would
never think of excluding males from the action, and en-
courage them to check out their act whenever they're in
town. On one occasion, Raul, Brody, David, and Dru
were surprised to receive a visit from an unlikely fan.
"In Miami, we had this huge guy with a fistful of beer,

looking like he rode in on a Harley, wait in line for an hour for our autograph," Dru revealed to the *Knight Ridder* newspaper. "We're up there for the fellas, too."

During another routine outing, Raul, Brody, David, and Dru spotted some guys grooving to their song on the radio. They were so happy to see male fans embrace their music that they decided to share in a manly bonding moment. "The best feeling was we were driving the other day and a car drove up going the opposite way," Raul recounted the incident to America Online. "Our song was on the radio and they came and the guys in the car were singing in the car and we were like, 'That's our song! Yeah!' And it was guys too, which to us it's like cool, dude, 'cause it's all about the guys."

While being the object of so many fans' affections can be flattering, the guys of C-Note have already had their share of strange fan encounters. One time a girl convinced them that her father owned the hotel where the group would be staying. After following the group in her car, she arrived at the hotel, only to be discredited by the hotel manager.

Although other equally strange incidents have been known to happen, the guys would never think of discouraging their fans. In fact, no matter how weird things seem to get sometimes, the group is happy to have the kind of fan base that's loyal enough to go out of their way to meet them. "There's been a smart group of fans that, instead of waiting at the exit, like everybody else does, they waited in their car around the corner and spotted out for the limo," Raul explained during an online chat. "They saw which one we got into and followed us back to the hotel. So actually when we saw they had gone through all that trouble just to meet us, we said, okay, we got out and said you didn't have to go through all that and applauded them."

No matter how good it feels, all of this fame and recognition can, at times, be difficult to deal with. But getting chased through alleys, finding fans in hotel rooms, and having to be escorted out of concerts is something that C-Note has yet to experience. Unlike most pop groups, who are tired of playing the cat-and-mouse game, the guys of C-Note are actually looking forward to a time when they, too, can lay claim to this pop music rite of passage. "We're still pretty new to this, so we want the mobs of fans," Brody admitted to *Teen* magazine. "We want people to come running after us, we want to be escorted from the building!"

Fame is all well and good, but too much of this good thing, and even the most grounded of individual stands in danger of getting carried away by the hype mobile. Luckily the guys of C-Note don't have that problem. No matter how famous they get or how many autographs they sign, they vowed early on that they would never take their success for granted. In fact, the guys are always on ego-patrol with one another, making sure that the group has all of its feet on the ground at all times.

For the C-Note four, the most effective reality check is to remember where they came from and all of the struggles they'd had to endure along the way. "I don't think you'll find four more levelheaded guys," Raul remarked to Gavin.com. "That goes all the way back to when we were all working two jobs and finding time to rehearse at our parents' houses three or four times a week. We know we're very blessed right now. There's no reason to be big-headed."

Besides, if any of the guys ever required an ego deflation, they'd need only to visit their family and old friends, who never let the fab four forget about who they really are. And although everyone is impressed with their success back home, they would never let them get caught up in the glitz and glamour of the music business. "If our heads start to get big, our parents will call us on it right away," Brody told *Latin Girl* magazine.

When you add the fact that Brody, David, Dru, and Raul are extremely spiritual, it becomes difficult to imagine any of them ever losing sight of what's important in life. Whether they're making a video, recording their album, or performing on stage, the guys are amazed with the cards life has dealt them. They feel so blessed by the turn their lives have taken, that they are always thanking the powers that be for bringing them together. "We like to say that fate brought us together," explained Brody. "Everything happens for a reason. Something higher than us is guiding this."

HIGHER AND HIGHER

No matter how mature or down-to-earth some people may be, you can bet that the chance to appear on television will bring out the little kid in them. When C-Note found out that they would be singing on nationally broadcast television shows, all of their media-trained polish went right out the nearest window. In fact, when the guys were first informed that they would be singing on *The Rosie O'Donnell Show* on May 25, they were sailing on cloud nine and dreaming of the big day for weeks.

As one of the most popular daytime talk shows, *The Rosie O'Donnell Show* has consistently featured the best of the best in the music industry. Being invited to sing on Rosie's famed stage was a dream come true. Add to that the fact that the group would have their largest audience to date, and it's easy to see why C-Note was thoroughly blissed out by the opportunity.

When the guys arrived at the show, they were ushered into the green room where they chatted with other celebrity guests and munched on the appetizing food. Then, after what seemed like hours, the moment they had been waiting for arrived—the show's producer popped in to give them their cue. Their time to take the stage was finally upon them.

As soon as Rosie introduced the group, the audience went wild. Dressed in sleek, black cargo pants and button-down shirts, the guys' striking good looks had everyone in a tizzy. And when they brought down the house, showing that they could sing and dance even better than they looked, the auditorium broke out in deafening applause.

For all their preshow jitters, the guys came off looking as if they had been doing the TV show circuit all of their lives.

People who had never seen the group before smiled and clapped with all the enthusiasm of fervent 'N Sync fans. Judging by the looks on their faces, Raul, David, Brody, and Dru were extremely satisfied with the caliber of the performance that day. Calling the guys "cuties" and grinning from ear to ear, Rosie O'Donnell herself seemed to have been smitten with the fine young crooners.

After getting Rosie's seal of approval, the guys had no problem going head-to-head with either Jenny Jones's or Ricki Lake's studio audience. Going by all the cheers and catcalls that emanated from the crowd, it's clear that C-Note's hard-core fans turned out in large numbers to get a good look at the guys who'd stolen their hearts. Indeed, when they performed the hit single, it was all the hosts could do to keep fans from rushing the stage.

Having begun auspiciously enough with *The Rosie O'Donnell Show*, the round of televised appearances came to a grand finale when the guys were booked to sing on one of daytime's most popular soap operas, *All My Children*. On June 8, 1999, the boys taped an episode in which they performed at the S.O.S. Club, a popular hangout for the characters on the show. Although their primary role was to sing, the guys had to learn the ins and outs of the acting business—and fast. After shooting one take after another, David, Brody, Raul, and Dru gained a whole new respect for the actors who work so long and hard to bring viewers their daily dose of daytime melodrama.

TOURING THE COUNTRY

Whenever the guys would stop to reflect on how far their group had come in the last year alone, they never failed to get blown away by all that they'd accomplished and learned on their climb to the stars. It seemed as if nothing could top their many television appearances, magazine features, and radio interviews—until, that is, they were invited to join the all-star lineup on Brandy's "Never Say Never" summer tour.

For all intents and purposes, getting this primo gig was just about the best thing that could happen to an up-and-coming group like C-Note. For all the promotion and exposure, the guys were still a fledgling ensemble. Although they would have loved to launch a full-scale, large venue tour and improve their album sales, they had yet to develop the kind of following that could fill stadiums. So what were they to do? Playing smaller clubs would get their names out there, but it wouldn't give them as much exposure as a concert tour. Thus, when Brandy's people approached C-Note about joining her caravan of summer fun, the group was only too psyched to come onboard.

Just as the guys were beginning to think that their prospects couldn't get any brighter, another superstar gave them something to believe in. Cher, who was planning to launch her first stateside tour for the chart-topping *Believe* album, contacted the group about opening for her during a couple of shows. Well, this was indeed something unusual. Most groups don't get to warm up an audience for such a renowned pop icon until much later on in their careers. But, of course, C-Note would break all the rules in their journey to the top of the charts. "We're really looking forward to seeing the show, we really are," Raul told MTV. "We don't know what it's going to be, but we're really looking forward to just being on the same bill with [Cher]."

While Brandy's tour would help them amass younger

fans, being on tour with Cher would expose the group to an audience that wouldn't normally listen to their brand of music. The chance to make an impact on a whole new group of people was almost as exciting as being on tour with the diva herself. "[We're looking forward] to always broadening our audience, too," Dru explained to MTV. "Especially with somebody like Cher, she's got a lot of the older crowd, and that's going to be interesting."

Whatever happened next, one thing was for certain: David, Raul, Brody, and Dru were about to have the summer of their lives. "June 18 we'll be on tour with Brandy, and Tyrese is on that tour and Silk is on the tour. And it's going from June 18 to August 2 and then Cher starts a little bit after that. So all summer long we'll be booking and going out with Brandy and Cher."

Recent years have seen C-Note developing in leaps and bounds. From their early days as a Spanish language group to their struggles as a bilingual anomaly to their unbelievable breakthrough into the hearts and minds of America's music lovers, the guys never let doubt and fear dictate their actions. Today, C-Note's days of worrying about the future are a thing of the past—replaced by boundless confidence and undying optimism. And who could blame Raul, Brody, David, and Dru for being so chipper? In a couple of years' time they have managed to break cultural barriers and unite fans from every conceivable walk of life in the name of one common cause.

They are now enjoying the very success they'd striven so hard to attain. Appearing on television shows, meeting fans from all over the country, shooting music videos, and getting the chance to work with some of the industry's leading musicians is what every group wants, but C-Note dared to go the distance and achieve what so many had said was impossible, impractical, and unattainable.

Like anybody whose wildest dreams have become business as usual, the guys are eternally grateful to all the people who helped them rise to the top, and, most important, the fans who have given them a reason to sing.

11

The Star Connection

While astrology has its fair share of detractors, there are those who would swear by its powers to predict the future and explain the inexplicable. When it comes to getting to know your favorite pop group, nothing beats reading up on the guys' sun signs. Sure, you can find out all the vital statistics like where they were born, their height, and even favorite TV show just by leafing through a magazine, but when it comes to the nitty-gritty, their most hidden personality traits, the signs of the zodiac never lie.

BRODY

Pisces (February 21–March 20)
As a Pisces, Brody is under one of the most compassionate and giving signs of the zodiac. His first priority is to help his fellow human beings, and he will go out of his way for family and friends. The Pisces sign also endows Brody with keen insight, allowing him to sense what his friends and loved ones are thinking. People often do not live up to his expectations. But since Brody tries to focus on people's positive traits rather than their

flaws, he can maintain harmonious relationships with everyone he meets.

In matters of the heart, Pisces tend to get disappointed, often ending up giving more than they receive. For Brody, the key to making relationships work is to find someone who won't take advantage of his generosity. When feelings are hurt, the Pisces has a hard time withdrawing from the relationship. But once they do, their ex can forget about getting them back. They are just as slow to forgive as they are to get angry. As a hopeless romantic and someone who's capable of feeling great love, the Pisces male is bound to find an everlasting love that's custom-made for the storybooks.

Brody's sign also shows that he is very neat, meticulous, and has an overriding fondness for order. You won't catch him trying to challenge his best buds. Retiring and humble, Brody would rather people-watch from the sidelines than get involved in all the action. Sometimes his lack of self-confidence can get the better of him, but once he matures, the Pisces sign will inevitably become more self-assured and successful.

One of the most misunderstood signs of the zodiac, a Pisces personality is very hard to pin down. One minute they're talking a mile a minute to their best friend, the next they're retreating into a corner at a party. Pisces have a tendency of changing their mood on a frequent basis, leaving people in constant perplexity. But if anyone enjoys being a mystery, it's the Pisces. People born of this sign value their privacy above all else, and can alienate people by acting aloof and withdrawn.

When it comes to the arts, Brody is a typical Pisces. Highly imaginative, artistic, and creative, he loves writing poetry and dabbling with song lyrics. Escaping into a world of imagination is one of Pisces's favorite pastimes, and Brody is lucky in that he can make a living doing what he loves best—writing and singing songs. Pisces shun logic, and rightly so. For them, there is no higher order than the imagination, and once they tap into their powers of creativity, there is nothing that can stop them from achieving greatness.

Soul Mates: Cancer, Scorpio, Pisces

Great Chemistry: Aries, Taurus, Capricorn, Aquarius

Fifty-fifty: Leo, Libra

Better Luck with the Next Guy: Gemini, Virgo, Sagittarius

DAVID

Virgo (August 21–September 20)

David's quick wit, professionalism, and ambition make him the quintessential Virgo. People born under this sign are naturally contemplative and are quick to acquire new skills. Things that take most people a while to learn, Virgo can pick up in minutes. David is also very philosophical. He prefers to think about the bigger picture. But don't for one minute think that he can't be practical when he wants to. Virgos are ruthless negotiators, and usually get their way in any situation. Of course, David would rather use reason than force to make his point. Endowed with an innate appreciation for the rational and logical, he is a skilled debater on any subject.

David is also blessed with Virgo's exacting streak of perfectionism. He will work for hours—even days—to get something right. He is also a very harsh critic of himself and others, expecting people to live up to his high ideals and standards. Although he will never take a backseat in the game of life, David's sign is prone to worry about the future. Anxieties about wealth, success, and power occupy his mind to the point where he is sometimes unsure of whether he will achieve his goals. That's why Virgos need to stay active. Spending their time worrying about their life's course is the last thing they want to do.

When it comes to boredom, no one hates it more than a Virgo. David would rather have too much to do than not enough. In fact, he always makes sure that he's over-extended, just in case he runs out of activities to occupy his mind. Virgos are one of the most hardworking signs of the zodiac, and their attention to detail helps them succeed in any profession.

As a Virgo, David also has a very active imagination, as well as a fondness for the finer things in life, like music and literature. Yet, unlike David, most Virgos don't pursue a career in the arts, for fear of not being able to make a living. As an earth sign, Virgos prefer stability, but they can also quickly adapt to change if the need should arise.

To their friends, Virgos appear to be flexible and easy-going. But deep inside, they have a constant meter running, tallying up all of the flaws and good qualities of their mates. And even when Virgos seem to be going with the flow, they are keeping track of everything, from where they're going to how they will get there.

In relationships, David can be overly analytic and critical. But these personality traits shouldn't be confused with a cold heart. Virgos are just looking for that perfect partner to share their life with. And because he is not flirtatious by nature, David believes in quality over quantity. If you want to win this guy's affections, your best bet is to be honest and not play games. A Virgo can spot a lie a mile away, and prefers to share his life with someone who is practical and sensible like himself.

Soul Mates: Capricorn, Taurus, Virgo

Great Chemistry: Libra, Scorpio, Cancer, Leo

Fifty-fifty: Aquarius, Aries

Better Luck with the Next Guy: Sagittarius, Pisces, Gemini

RAUL

Taurus (April 21–May 20)

Although he seems fiery and unpredictable to his many fans, there is nothing spontaneous about Raul. For this earth sign of the zodiac, it's all in the Ps—practicality, predictability, and preparation. You won't find a Taurus chasing some unattainable pipe dream. For Tauruses to pursue something to its full extent, they have to think everything through and calculate the profits they stand to gain. With his feet planted firmly on the ground, Raul is always levelheaded and immersed in thoughts about the future.

While some astrologers are quick to say that Taurus is materialistic, this sign actually has one of the healthiest attitudes toward money. Sure, Tauruses want to have enough money and even work steadily to build a solid foundation. But it's not greed that drives their acquisitive natures so much as a love for the finer things in life. Raul is no exception. He can be very discriminating when it comes to choosing the right clothes, listening to the right music, and eating the best food. Connoisseurs of every luxury item available, Tauruses have a natural fondness for the best money can buy.

This sensuality extends to other areas in their life as well. Taurus is a very physical sign—they like to express their feelings by touching, hugging, and kissing. Words leave them cold; but give them a long back rub and they'll find a way to return the favor.

When it comes to finding a suitable partner, Taurus can be very critical. Just as they appreciate the finer things in life, they also want to find the best possible match, and will never settle for second best. Once they do find the person of their dreams, Tauruses can be romantic and emotional.

"Stubborn" is another word that comes into play when describing a Taurus. As the bull in the zodiac, they are prone to argue just for the sake of argument. But these debates are all in good fun. People under this sign are not ones to get angered quickly, but once they see red, watch out—they can become fierce competitors.

The Taurus in Raul also makes him resistant to change. Whether it's choosing a new ice-cream flavor or moving to a new city, Tauruses hate to have their routine disrupted. Like all earth signs, they thrive on stability and prefer to hang around people with the same needs.

Being both the most true blue of friends and the most dreaded of enemies, Tauruses are very loyal to their comrades, often going above and beyond the call of duty. Nor do they care if their friends don't always reciprocate in kind. For Raul, giving is always more fun than receiving. People who are lucky enough to befriend Raul are always talking about his generosity and honesty.

Soul Mates: Virgo, Taurus, Capricorn

Great Chemistry: Gemini, Cancer, Pisces, Aries

Fifty-fifty: Libra, Sagittarius

Better Luck with the Next Guy: Aquarius, Leo, Scorpio

DRU

Cancer (June 21–July 20)

Dru may seem confident and pulled together onstage, but when he's not putting his best foot forward for the spectators, he can be extremely insecure and sensitive. Bouncing back from an insult is very difficult for this sign, and wounds of the past can take many years to heal.

Cancers don't tend to forgive and forget very easily, either. But that's because they feel the pains of everyday life much more keenly than other signs. Although they may show a brave face to the world, Cancers are prone to depression and feelings of inadequacy. Even when the world is at their feet, people born under this sign have a hard time looking at the bright side.

Because Dru can be hypersensitive, he requires the support of good friends and loving mentors. Judging by the support network that his fellow C-Noters and Trans Con family provide, Dru is one lucky guy. It is because he is so supported and respected by these people that he can go on stage with the confidence of a seasoned performer.

One of Cancer's best qualities is the importance he or she places on building a family. A Cancer thrives within small, tight-knit groups, and seeks out the stability that can be found in a rich family life. Once Dru finds a group he is comfortable with, there are no bounds to his loyalty. He will bend over backward to make sure that his friends and family are happy.

Another common trait of Cancers is their inability to put the past behind them. All Cancers love to get nostalgic, even when it's about a situation that went horribly wrong in the past. Reminiscing can be an enjoyable pastime, but Cancers often dredge up bad memories that keep them from fully enjoying the present moment.

As a Cancer, Dru craves a deep, everlasting love, but fears he will never find it. In a relationship, Cancers can be extremely moody and self-conscious. They have a tendency to put their partners on a pedestal, whether or not they deserve to be placed there. Even though they crave stability, they are often attracted to unpredictable and adventurous people. In the end, however, Cancers become too possessive of their partners, and can be overly demanding. One of the most ideal partners in the right relationship, Cancers can make love work, provided they find someone who appreciates their sensitivity, love of order, and kindness.

For all their insecurities and hesitancy, Cancers love the limelight. More than anything else, they seek recognition and a loyal following. It seems that Dru is one Cancer who has gotten his wish in spades.

Soul Mates: Scorpio, Pisces

Great Chemistry: Leo, Virgo, Taurus, Gemini

Fifty-fifty: Sagittarius, Aquarius

Better Luck with the Next Guy: Libra, Capricorn, Aries, Cancer

12

Test Your C-Note IQ

If you think you know everything there is to know about C-Note, now is your chance to prove it. Just grab a pen and fill out the following quiz to the best of your ability. Then, compare your results with those of your friends. Let the best C-Note fan win!

1. *Which member was born in San Juan, Puerto Rico?*

   A. Brody
   B. Dru
   C. David
   D. Raul

2. *On what day did the group release their debut album?*

   A. May 28, 1999
   B. June 25, 1999
   C. May 25, 1999
   D. June 29, 1999

3. *Who is the only member who doesn't have a pet?*

   A. David
   B. Raul
   C. Brody
   D. Dru

4. *In what city did C-Note get its start?*

   A. Boston
   B. New York
   C. Orlando
   D. Miami

5. *Which C-Note member wears glasses/contacts?*

   A. Brody
   B. David
   C. Raul
   D. Dru

6. *How many members are of Hispanic background?*

   A. 1
   B. 2
   C. 3
   D. 4

7. *Which two members played basketball in high school?*

   A. Raul and Brody
   B. Dru and Raul
   C. Brody and Dru
   D. David and Raul

8. *On which television show has C-Note not made an appearance?*

   A. Soul Train
   B. Rosie O'Donnell

C. Jerry Springer
D. Jenny Jones

9. *Which record label gave C-Note its first recording contract?*

A. Sony
B. Epic
C. Universal
D. Motown

10. *On which soap opera was C-Note invited to sing?*

A. *General Hospital*
B. *As the World Turns*
C. *Days of Our Lives*
D. *All My Children*

11. *Which song did C-Note help write?*

A. "Spanish Fly"
B. "Wait Till I Get Home"
C. "I Like"
D. "So Often"

12. *Which producer did* not *work on* A Different Kind of Love*?*

A. Guy Rocke
B. Dakari
C. Babyface
D. Ginuwine

13. *Which member grew up in Hoboken, New Jersey?*

A. Raul
B. David
C. Dru
D. Brody

14. Which famous celebrity did Raul imitate as a young boy?

   A. Billy Idol
   B. Rick Springfield
   C. John Travolta
   D. Sylvester Stallone

15. Which C-Note member is Stevie Wonder's biggest fan?

   A. Dru
   B. David
   C. Brody
   D. Raul

ANSWER KEY

1. A	4. C	7. D	10. D	13. B
2. C	5. A	8. C	11. A	14. C
3. B	6. C	9. B	12. C	15. A

FIVE AND BELOW: In Need of C-Notes

And you call yourself a fan! Some studying up on your C-Note trivia is in order. Not to worry, though: There are plenty of ways for you to get your daily dose of C-Note sustenance and bring yourself up to a level of fandom that would make any of the guys proud! There are tons of C-Note websites sprouting up every day (see chapter 13 for some of the best), and as the guys get more and more popular, television, radio, and magazines work hard to keep up with the demand from their growing fan base. And, of course, you can keep this book on your bedside table for quick reference to your most burning C-Note questions. So there's no reason for you to be so C-Note illiterate. Get off your buns and get to work!

SIX TO ELEVEN CORRECT ANSWERS: Getting Closer to Home...

You're wild about *A Different Kind of Love* and you probably have a favorite band member, but clearly your C-Note knowledge is not quite up to par. You know the words to "Wait Till I Get Home" by heart, but the rest of the album is sort of a blur of smooth sounds and sexy voices. You're familiar with the guys' backgrounds and interests, but could you pick out Brody's voice from, say, David's? Perhaps you've spread yourself too thin in your fan adoration—and with good reason. Between the Backstreet Boys, 'N Sync, and the rest of the Trans Con family, it's hard to keep up on the latest info for all of them. But if you're interested in following the guys as they continue to climb to the top, just a *little* more effort is needed. Listen to that CD a bit more closely from now on, browse those websites every couple of days, join the fan club, and you're on your way to total C-Note devotion!!!

TWELVE AND ABOVE: Your Heart and Soul Belong to C-Note

A true C-Note fan, your limitless knowledge of the band is to be admired. You probably belong to the fan club, have been to every C-Note meet-and-greet within a five-state radius, own two copies of their hot debut CD (one for home and one for your Discman), have your walls plastered with the sweet smiles of Dru and Raul, and actively try to convert your friends into C-Note fanatics as well. You know everything there is to know about these hotties—heck, you probably know the guys better than they know themselves! And who could blame you? Performers as talented and adorable as the guys in C-Note don't just grow on trees. Every time you look at their pictures, every time you hear their voices, every time you watch them move, your heart melts. You are an incurable C-Note romantic, and a fan the guys are certain to be eternally grateful to have.

13

Cyber C-Note

As the freshest thing to hit the United States since the invention of the ceiling fan, C-Note's presence on the World Wide Web has gone from nonexistent to total domination. When its first album was released on May 25, 1999, the group boasted a total of five sites. Only a few months later, fans from all over the world were getting in on the cyber action by paying their own tributes to the group. The group currently has fifteen fan websites and clubs to their name, and that's just for starters.

Whether you're interested in checking out hot pictures of the guys, posting your thoughts on the clubs and message boards, reading up on the latest C-Note news and concerts, or listening to their soulful music, you'll find everything you need and more in the following fan sites. So point your mouse, click to these awesome sites, and enjoy a complete, interactive C-Note experience.

OFFICIAL C-NOTE PAGE
http://www.cnote.com

There was a time when the official site was little more than a couple of photos and a few news bytes. But much like C-Note, this site has come a long way. Its new colorful look brings in thousands of hits per day. And who could blame fans for flocking to this awesome site? Log on and you'll find yourself overwhelmed by all of the options available. You can also enter to win a Play Station, check out the latest news, read the guys' biographies, and see a video of them making their debut album. Still not convinced? Then head on over to the multimedia area where you'll find enough pictures, sounds, and downloads to keep you busy for hours on end. Then head on over to the schedule area so you can check when C-Note is coming to a town near you.

Final Grade: A+

C-NOTE CRAZED
http://www.come.to/cnote

Take just one look at this mega C-Note emporium and you'll know why Kristie, the creator, is considered to be C-Note's most devoted fan. Not only was she one of the first to create a C-Note web tribute, but she's been working nonstop to perfect and redesign her site. Well, the results just couldn't be any better. The sleek and lively opening page provides a frames and nonframes option, and once you get inside, prepare to spend some time. You'll need every minute to explore the many exciting features that this winning site offers. Here you'll find a discography, track listings, lyrics to all of C-Note's wonderful songs, downloads, pictures of the guys in concert and in the studio, a tour schedule, TV/radio appearances, magazine articles, a place to adopt a C-Noter, fan experiences, cool C-Note links, and even a pen pal area. A must-see for any true fan of C-Note.

Final Grade: A

THE FIRST UNOFFICIAL C-NOTE PAGE
http://www.angelfire.com/oh2/cnote/

The dynamic duo behind this one-of-a-kind website deserves a hearty pat on the back for a job well done. Highly organized and painstakingly maintained, this page boasts a wealth of great information on C-Note. What's also really cool about this site is that just like the group itself, the creators offer a Spanish version. Included in this incredible site are sections devoted to news, lyrics, tour schedule, obsession signs, lyrics, articles, secret rumors, loads of multimedia, fun photo gallery of the guys, a review of their video, famous quotes, chat transcripts, lookalikes, contests, a message board, and a C-Note store. So stop on by, and get hooked on C-Note for life.
Final Grade: A−

THE C-NOTE EXPERIENCE
http://listen.to/c-note

As a late entry into the cyber C-Note community, this site is already off to a great start. Among its arsenal of features, you'll find concert pictures, C-Note schedule, biographies of our favorite guys, lyrics, a "You Know You're Obsessed When . . ." section, discography, downloads, and concert experiences. With a great start like this, there's no telling what the creator will think up next. Look for many great things from this site in the future.
Final Grade: B

THE C-NOTE VIBE
http://www.geocities.com/TimesSquare/Tower/2727/

A one-stop C-Note shop is what you'll get when you surf your way over to this awe-inspiring web tribute. The reason for all this fuss? You have to see it to believe it. With its colorful background, clean layout, and plentiful information, this is one site you simply can't afford to miss. You'll find a complete C-Note history, a news page, individual biographies, media, downloads, a quiz, magazine articles, links, trading post, tour schedule, and a whole lot more. But don't take my word for it, check it out for yourself. You'll be glad you did.

Final Grade: A+

C-NOTE & YOU DON'T STOP!
http://cnotefan.cjb.net

One of the best sites on C-Note today, this site has barrels of info on the fabulous foursome. Easy to navigate and quick to load, it is also regularly maintained. Judging by how many hits it has received, it is by far one of the most popular stops on the C-Note cyber tour. This site features magazine articles, news, polls, contact information, schedule, and one of the most complete multimedia sections on the entire World Wide Web. It is a veritable treasure trove of everything C-Note, so get in on the action now!

Final Grade: A−

C-NOTE: CAN'T WAIT 'TIL THEY GET HOME
http://www.geocities.com/Tokyo/Gulf/3063/

Although it has one of the best appearances of all the sites, this site could benefit from a little more substance. After all, inquiring minds do want to know all about C-Note. But lest you think this page is all glitz, think again. You'll find plenty to view here, including cool pics of the guys, downloads, a news page, and a complete schedule. Stop on by and show your support by signing the webmaster's guestbook.

Final Grade: B−

BOYBAND UNIVERSE-C-NOTE
*http://www.geocities.com/SunsetStrip/Plaza/8950/
main.html*

With their own great page dedicated to them, C-Note
has found a permanent home in the Boyband Universe.
It is located alongside other stand-out groups like Backstreet Boys and 'N Sync; you will be able to get all the
goods on the favorite four, as well as on the other Trans
Con sensations. Look out for individual profiles, transcripts, articles, message board, news, schedule, an ex-
haustive image gallery. With all of these things going
for it, the creator should take some time to spice up the
site's overall image. Other than that, this website is a
real winner.
Final Grade: B

C-NOTE
http://www.geocities.com/SunsetStrip/Disco/8127

It may not have everything your heart desires, but it is
still a nice effort by a loyal C-Note fan. Here you'll find
sounds, FAQs, a regularly updated schedule, and pictures galore. The clean design and professional look
earns this site extra credit.
Final Grade: B—

EPIC—C-NOTE
*http://www.epicrecords.com/EpicCenter/custom/
1079*

Great site from the people who gave C-Note their record
deal. Let's all show them that they made the right decision by logging on whenever possible. Once you click
your way to this awesome site, you can read all the latest
news, download a video profile, sign up for C-Note's
mailing list, or send a friend a C-Note musicgram. Now
if that's not what good friends are for, what is?
Final Grade: A

C-NOTE WORLDWIDE
http://members.theglobe.com/cnww/index.htm

This feast for the eyes includes tons of information for you to read and enjoy. The site features track listings, news, photos, a place to chat, fan experiences, audio, C-Note wallpaper downloads, biographies, and more. Do yourself a favor and bookmark this page. You never know when the urge to surf will strike.

Final Grade: B+

PLANET C-NOTE
http://www.geocities.com/Hollywood/Club/9949/ pcnframes.html

Let's hear it for the boys. This site makes a very powerful statement about C-Note. With its ultra-cool background and meticulous organization, it is a must-see for any C-Note devotee. Cruise on over and discover the gallery of pictures, full group and member bios, a complete discography including the creator's review, and tons of links.

Final Grade: B

C-NOTE...FEELS SO GOOD
http://www.angelfire.com/ga2/CNoteFeelsSoGood/ index.html

This page is on its way to becoming a real contender. It sports a nice design, but will have a better chance of enticing fans with new features and additional sections. As it stands, this site offers member biographies, TV appearances, tour schedule, and links. With a little more work, this site will be one for the record books.

Final Grade: B−

C-NOTE LOVE PAGE
*http://www.geocities.com/Broadway/Orchestra/
1741/*

Judging by the title, the webmaster of this site is obviously head over heels in love with C-Note. But in the game of love, words are cheap. That's why this creator puts her effort where her mouth is, crafting a site that is both fun and functional. A vibrant background and clean layout sets off the somewhat limited amount of info nicely.

Final Grade: B—

Elina Furman is the author of numerous books, some of which include: *Ricky Martin, James Van Der Beek, The Heat Is On: 98°, Give It to You: The Jordan Knight Story, The Everything After College Book, Generation Inc., Heart of Soul: The Lauryn Hill Story,* and *The Everything Dating Book.* She lives and works in Chicago, Illinois.

CELEBRITIES YOU WANT TO READ ABOUT